ENCHANTED DESERT

A strange man takes Cindy Charles from a jeweller's in London's Bond Street to the deserts of Saudi Arabia. The man, an Arab with green eyes, is Sheikh Al Adham. He is handsome with an air of mystery that the flowing robes of Arabia emphasise . . . At the first opportunity, Cindy escapes the influence of the man whom she finds so disturbing. But on reaching England she finds him impossible to forget. And then Cindy is sent on a straightforward journey, which has an unexpected meeting in store for her.

ISOBEL SCOTT

ENCHANTED DESERT

Complete and Unabridged

LINFORD
Leicester

First published in Great Britain in 1981 by
Robert Hale Limited
London

First Linford Edition
published 2006
by arrangement with
Robert Hale Limited
London

British Library CIP Data

Scott, Isobel
    Enchanted desert.—Large print ed.—
Linford romance library
1. Love stories
2. Large type books
I. Title
823.9′14 [F]

ISBN 1–84617–221–7

Published by
F. A. Thorpe (Publishing)
Anstey, Leicestershire

Set by Words & Graphics Ltd.
Anstey, Leicestershire
Printed and bound in Great Britain by
T. J. International Ltd., Padstow, Cornwall

This book is printed on acid-free paper

1

'Oh, Miss Charles, Mr Gascoigne would like to see you in his office as soon as possible.'

The girl swung round from her workdesk just in time to see the door close behind Miss Grange, Mr Gascoigne's private secretary but even the brief glimpse was sufficient for the disapproval to register. Cindy sighed as she uncurled herself from the tall stool and stood up. After nearly five months with the famous Bond Street firm of Daubeny and Gascoigne she was no nearer breaking through the icy reserve of Madeleine Grange. And as luck would have it, up here on the top floor, they were the only two women employees.

There were all the men in the workroom, of course, but it would have been pleasant to have a friend of one's

1

own sex. Downstairs in the showroom there were several girls but ground floor staff arrived and left at different times from the workroom employees and that in itself appeared to constitute a barrier.

Cindy turned back to her table, hastily covered her drawings and reached for her handbag. As soon as possible, Miss Grange had said. She had better go and tidy her face and then hurry along to the boss's office.

It took her only a few minutes to run a comb through her long hair and to brush her eyebrows with a damp finger. She saw in the mirror that her cheeks had a slight flush indicating her nervousness and as she walked along the deeply carpeted corridor, she took several long breaths in an effort to calm down.

'Just go in, Miss Charles.' Miss Grange didn't lift her eyes from her typewriter as the girl walked into her room and the casual query that Cindy had prepared was never made. There was no point she thought in asking

Madeleine Grange if she had any idea what the boss wanted. For Mr Gascoigne was Mr Gascoigne, and words like the boss or the chief might as soon be applied to God himself as to Mr Gascoigne.

'You wished to see me Mr Gascoigne?' Cindy walked over the deep carpet, deeper even than the one in the corridor and didn't speak until she reached the edge of the large desk.

'Ah, yes, Cindy.' The rather short-sighted eyes looked up at her, he waved her to a seat and returned his attention to the papers on his desk. 'I'll just finish these letters and then I'll be with you.'

She watched while he put his signature at the foot of all the pages without appearing to read them and listened while he spoke to his secretary in the outer office on the internal phone.

'Yes I've finished with the letters Miss Grange, if you'd like to come in now.'

There was scarcely a sound as the

door opened and Miss Grange came across the room to pick up the papers. And there was scarcely a sound as she murmured something extremely confidential in Mr Gascoigne's ear. Cindy saw the look of blankness on his face replaced by dawning perception.

'Oh, yes, of course. The fish. I hadn't forgotten Miss Grange, but thank you for reminding me.' Suddenly he smiled at the girl sitting on the far side of the desk. 'What would men like me do without our secretaries, Cindy? I should have been in trouble at home if I had gone leaving the sole in the office.'

Cindy murmured something but she could see from the firmness about Miss Grange's mouth that she had not welcomed his divulgence of her message. Impatiently Cindy waited for the final collection of all the papers, the last fussy little touch to the blotting pad before Miss Grange turned and walked quickly across the room. Although Cindy wasn't looking at her, she could see the angry glint of Miss Grange's eyes behind the glasses. And she knew that she was not pleased.

'Well, Cindy.' Mr Gascoigne leaned forward on his desk. 'Tell me, how are things going?'

'Very well, thank you, Mr Gascoigne.' Cindy's reply was reluctant. She knew that she hadn't been summoned to the boss's office just to answer rhetorical questions. Especially when he had asked and she had answered the very same one last week. At length. When she had signed a permanent employment contract at the end of her four month trial period. She waited. Watched him pick up his spectacles from the desk and polish them.

'Are you going out tonight, Cindy?'

'Going out?' Foolishly she repeated the question. Then, because she couldn't think of any reason for avoiding the truth, 'No, I don't have anything planned.' When she had spoken, she had a sudden sense of misgiving. Suppose, she thought wildly, suppose he asked her to go out with him. She had heard he was a bit of a philanderer. Of course she hadn't believed it, who would? But it just could be true. Hypnotised she looked at him and saw his lips move.

'That's good.' He was smiling as if he was a cat who had just swallowed the cream. 'Because there's something I would like you to do.' He paused and seemed to look for her immediate agreement.

'Yes. But I might . . . ' Feverishly she wondered if she could invent a boy-friend who had hinted that he might call round at the flat.

'Yes.' Mr Gascoigne went on as if he hadn't been listening properly. 'I would like you to come back tonight. About seven-thirty.' He pressed his finger-tips together and beamed at her. 'Take a taxi home to your flat and that will give you the opportunity to change into something pretty . . . '

Her worst fears almost confirmed, Cindy looked at him with fascinated eyes. 'But Mr Gascoigne . . . '

'No, I insist, Cindy. Take a taxi there and back again. You can claim against petty cash tomorrow. You see these customers . . . '

'Customers?' It was the first mention there had been of those.

'Yes, that's what I was telling you, Cindy.' Clearly he was trying to be patient. 'You know from time to time we have . . . ' he paused and smiled mysteriously, ' . . . important customers who like to come and see the showroom when we are closed for normal business.'

'Yes, I have heard.' Cindy's relief was so great that she would have agreed to almost anything, but in fact she had heard that very occasionally customers of such wealth and importance came on the scene that not only Daubeny and Gascoigne but every other jeweller in New Bond Street was anxious to court their patronage. 'Yes, but . . . '

'But you're wondering why we want you in the showroom when normally the sales staff can do all that is necessary.'

'Yes.' Relief was clear in her voice. 'What do you want me to do, Mr Gascoigne?'

'Well, these customers,' again that mysterious and yet somehow confidential smile, 'as well as being interested in all the traditional styles of jewellery are keen to see what some of our brightest designers,' now there was an approving little nod, 'are producing. This could be a very important night, Cindy. Not merely for the firm. But probably even more, for you, my dear.'

'Oh!' The possibilities and the responsibility seemed suddenly so overwhelming that Cindy felt she had no strength to say any more.

'Yes, I can see you're now beginning to appreciate the situation.' He paused. 'So, may we expect you back here at the time I suggested?' He looked at his watch. 'That should give you plenty of time to . . . ' there was a waving little movement of one hand, ' . . . to do

8

whatever it is that young women do on these occasions. Of course,' suddenly he felt that he ought perhaps to curb his enthusiasm, 'nothing too extreme, you understand. If you're in any doubt about what to wear, then I'm sure Miss Cavendish downstairs will be happy to advise you.'

By this time Cindy had recovered her breath some-what and she smiled as, sensing dismissal, she rose from her chair. 'All right, Mr Gascoigne. I'll see her before I go. Was there anything else, sir?'

'No, no.' He got up from behind the desk and walked with her to the heavy wood door. 'Just go along to the workroom and look out some of your newest drawings, I think those ones we chose to form the nucleus of our Nefertiti collection. Yes,' he said thoughtfully, 'I think those might do very well.' Again he smiled and opened the door for her. 'I shall see you later then, Cindy. I'm certain you will enjoy the experience.'

Cindy's brief glance at Miss Grange was not returned. Apparently she was absorbed in the pile of papers which were on her desk and did not look up. But it was very obvious that she had heard Mr Gascoigne's last words and that she had put her own construction on them.

Although, thought Cindy with a slight giggle, she couldn't imagine just what that construction might be. Not without the gift of an overfertile imagination and Miss G. didn't look the type for that. But soon she dismissed all thoughts of Madeleine Grange from her mind and concentrated on the comparative luxury of going home to the flat by taxi. There was no doubt that it was very much more comfortable than travelling by tube and she wished that her salary would stretch to the harmless indulgence a little more often.

Since leaving Art School where she had specialised in silversmithing and gem-setting, she had found difficulty in managing on the more than generous terms that she had been offered in Daubeny and Gascoigne's. It was because of influence she had got the job; she knew too many of her fellow students who still hadn't found employment to make any mistake about that. No, of course she knew and she was grateful. But from time to time she wondered if she would have been wiser to try to find a position in the provinces instead of in London.

But when she had been offered the job, straight from College, she had jumped at it and been grateful to escape the awful threat of teaching which hung over every art graduate like a Sword of Damocles. Hideously expensive as the capital might be, she must try to remember what the likely alternative would be. She leaned forward as the taxi drew up at the large Victorian house and began to riffle through her handbag for the fare.

It would have been nicer if the hall and stairway didn't always have that dusty, dry smell that suggested ancient sofas and long undisturbed stair carpets. She ran up the two flights of stairs lightly, her eyes on the dingy red and green pattern of the thin haircord. The light from the tall, unwashed stained glass windows did little to brighten the general gloom.

But there were times Cindy reminded herself, especially after rainstorms when the windows had been washed clean and the sun shone, that the glass reflected light in a kaleidoscope of brightness. Then her artist's eye could find a positive pleasure in the approach to her home.

Home. She closed the door behind her and looked at what home was. A single room, fairly large and with a view, not much of one but a view nonetheless. She went over to the large window as if to assure herself that it hadn't gone and she looked over the small park in the centre of the square. Here the residents had the privilege of walking their dogs and airing their opinions on a Sunday morning. There were usually fewer cars then, too. With the shops in the area closed there was no need for parking on a Sunday.

Cindy sighed and turned back to the room. Thank goodness, she had tidied it this morning before she had left for work. Sometimes if she slept too long she didn't have the time and it was always a shock to throw open her front door and be met with an unmade divan bed and the unwashed bowl and spoon from her breakfast cereal.

But today it all looked very neat and . . . almost homely she decided. Although her mother hadn't agreed with that when she had come to see it before she had gone off to America.

'Oh, darling!' Her face had fallen when they walked inside. 'Is this the best you can do?' Then, seeing her daughter's crest-fallen expression, 'Oh, well, I'm sure things might be worse. And as you say, the rent is reasonable. And when we get some new covers for the divan.' But she had sighed almost imperceptibly.

Undoubtedly the cover which her mother had ordered to be made to measure and the matching tablecloth in a linen weave material the colour of crushed strawberries had gone some way to redeeming the drabness of the room. The round table, although old, probably even an antique, had had little to recommend it and was best covered, the stains and scars of the last hundred years hidden from view.

And she had been so enthusiastic about the improvement that she had gone wild and had smuggled in a pot of forbidden emulsion paint and roller and had spent an entire weekend giving the whole place a face lift. Now, she felt quite proud of it in a subdued way. The pale cinnamon of the walls made a good contrast for the divan and even looked all right with the carpet, a nondescript brown mixture. Some pictures on the walls, over the bed a collage she had made the first year at college, some lamps bought from a large chain store and with attractive shades, one rich bronze and another with a trendy 'art nouveau' look, all had combined to give the ordinary room an originality that betrayed the artistic bent of the occupant.

After she had eaten a hasty meal, Cindy went into the tiny bathroom, rejoicing in the gush of hot water from the shower. This and the equally minute kitchen were the main reasons why she had decided on the flat. Both 'conveniences' were no more than cupboards and no doubt broke every rule in the town planner's handbook but they were her own and not to be shared with anyone. Not for her the scurrying along corridors clutching her dressing-gown and sponge bag against her, only to scurry back a moment later when she found that one of the other residents had beaten her to the bathroom. And although the kitchen boasted only a two-burner electric hotplate, so far it had been adequate for all the entertaining she was likely to do.

When she had finished in the bathroom, Cindy stood looking inside the large Victorian wardrobe that served as her only storage space. Something black, Miss Cavendish had said, and Cindy had assured her that would present no difficulty. She had bought a black skirt only recently and it was only a case of deciding what to wear on top. She reached inside for the skirt. Black. Well it was mainly black and only had that broad border of embroidered wools just above the hemline.

Critically Cindy studied it, her trained eye approving the geometric design in dark reds and browns. Then with a decisive movement she tossed it on to the divan and began to search frantically for something else.

When she was ready, Cindy surveyed herself with critical approval. The midi-length skirt was cut on the bias and clung to her slender waist and hips before flaring slightly above black high-heeled boots. The blouse she had chosen was also black, but in a thin silky material that contrasted with the dull wool of the skirt and round her neck on a long slender gilt chain was a piece of jewellery she had designed herself.

The black ensemble was a dramatic foil for her own rather unusual colouring. Her hair was the colour of ripe wheat, a shade of dull gold so that the brown eyes came as a surprise. This evening they were touched with bronze eyeshadow and the dark lashes were long enough to sweep her cheek. She smiled, pleased with her attractive appearance and turning from the long mirror inside the wardrobe door, she reached for the intricately wrought earrings which matched her pendant.

* * *

When she entered the side door of the showroom, it was like going into another world from the familiar

17

upstairs one. In the normal course of events she used a different door entirely, one at the back of the building which took her directly to the workroom and it was possibly only the third time that she had been in the more glamorous part of the business where all the really important work was done.

At the far end of the glittering room she could see Mr Gascoigne deep in discussion with Miss Cavendish. Mr Debenham who had opened the security door for Cindy after first checking her identity on the closed circuit television screen, smiled at her in a fatherly sort of way and introduced her to the girl who was busily filing her nails under the pretext of tidying out a velvet lined drawer of gold chains.

'Marjorie.' Mr Debenham tut-tutted when he saw what she was doing and the girl with an apologetic shrug and a smile slipped the file away in the pocket of her dress. 'Sorry, Mr Debenham. I had just caught one of my nails when I

18

was hurrying to come back.'

'Well, don't let Mr Gascoigne see you. Now you know Miss Charles from the workroom, don't you?' He turned to Cindy. 'Miss Smith is one of our best young saleswomen.' He looked back at the other girl in mock disapproval. 'Although I sometimes wonder how she does it!'

Marjorie Smith showed no sign of being upset by the words of her senior colleague. Instead, her round pretty face split into a smile revealing small white teeth.

'Hello, Miss Charles.' She held out a hand and Cindy took it. 'I can't think why we haven't met before. Except that ... ' She paused until Mr Debenham was out of earshot, ' ... except that the company thinks that the two parts of the business are best kept apart. Oh, and I think I was on holiday when you first started.'

'Yes, otherwise I would have met you. Mr Gascoigne did bring me down to introduce me to what he calls the downstairs staff.'

'It's like Upstairs Downstairs isn't it?'

'Yes, except that I'm not sure that you're not thought of as the most important.'

'Oh, I don't know. We get the impression that it all depends on the designers.' She turned away from Cindy and gave some attention to the tray of chains. 'I suppose that's why you've been brought down tonight.'

'Yes.' Cindy watched the girl's deft movements as she arranged the jewellery and then flicked a velvet cloth over them. 'But I'm not certain what I'm supposed to be doing.'

'Oh, I should think . . . ' She replaced the tray in the storage unit behind her and closed the self-locking glass doors. ' . . . you won't have to do anything except that sometimes if the customers want a piece designed individually it's handy to have someone who can provide ideas.'

'Well . . . ' Cindy turned and looked across to where the other members of the staff were in an apparently intense discussion with Mr Gascoigne. ' . . . I hope that I'm not just going to spend the night hanging about aimlessly.'

'Oh, I shouldn't worry about that. You can always keep your eyes peeled to see that they don't pinch anything.'

'Pinch anything?' Cindy gave a gasp of amusement. 'I don't suppose customers who have the run of the shop are likely to do that.'

'No . . . ' There was doubt in the other girl's voice. 'But in this business there are all sorts of funny customers. I have a friend who works across in Hemmings and they had someone in the other week, someone they knew well and who was a good customer and one of the girls saw him slip a ring into his pocket. Luckily they had the internal security on at the time otherwise the assistant might not have been believed.'

'How awful!' Cindy was genuinely shocked. 'What did they do?'

'Do?' Marjorie shrugged. 'They didn't

do anything. The girl reported it immediately she saw it happen then a re-run of the tape confirmed. But he is such a good customer that they decided to do nothing about it. Only, he'll be watched pretty closely next time he comes into the shop. Who says,' she smiled impishly, 'that there isn't one law for the rich and one for the poor?'

'Certainly, when you put it like that,' Cindy began uncertainly.

'Anyway, I don't suppose it will happen here. The people coming tonight are as rich as Croesus.' She wrinkled her short nose mockingly. 'Arabs, you know.'

But before Cindy had time to absorb and comment on this interesting piece of information, Mr Gascoigne had come hurrying over to them. His habitually calm manner was distorted by a frown.

'Ah, Cindy . . . ' He nodded at her abstractedly. 'You've got to know Miss Smith, that's good.' He turned to Marjorie. 'Can you give her some idea what she should do, Miss Smith?' And when the other girl looked at him rather blankly, 'Oh, of course I don't mean that I expect her to sell anything, although,' he gave a short rueful smile, 'I believe it sometimes isn't necessary to sell. They are so keen to buy. But that's by the way.' The worried look came down over his face again. 'What I mean is just put Cindy in the picture about what usually happens.' He turned again to Cindy. 'And you've left out all those sketches, Cindy, where you can put your hand on them if you're asked to produce something?'

'Yes. They're in the top drawer of my desk, Mr Gascoigne.'

'That's all right then.' He stared at the piece of paper he was holding in his hand then looked over at his senior assistant. 'Oh, Mr Debenham . . . ' And he hurried across the room.

Marjorie shot a wickedly amused glance at Cindy. 'Poor old Gaskers.' Her voice was discreetly low. 'He always gets into a flap on these occasions. I remember last year, when the customers were about to leave one night, there was a wailing of sirens and a whole fleet of police cars screeched to a stop at the door. Someone had reported that there seemed to be people in the showroom and the whole of Scotland Yard was on our doorstep. Later it circulated through that the boss had forgotten to let the police know that we were doing business that night. By the way,' there was a subtle change of manner. 'How come he uses your Christian name? With everyone else he's most punctilious. Even young Jacky, the errand boy receives his full title.'

'Oh,' Cindy felt a faint warmth in her cheeks, 'he knows my family. Slightly.' The eyes she raised were apologetic. 'I suppose I got the job through influence.'

'Well, don't apologise, love. Just thank God for it.' Suddenly her flippant manner faded and Cindy turned round to see that Miss Cavendish was almost upon them. The older woman smiled approvingly at the two girls.

'Marjorie, I'm glad you're helping Cindy. And you my dear . . . ' She surveyed the tall fair figure from top to toe. 'You look charming. When I said black I don't know that I had anything quite so glamorous in mind. But never mind, you'll do very well if only you don't distract attention from what we're trying to sell.' She walked past them towards one of the glittering show cases near the front of the shop.

'Oh, dear.' Again Cindy felt the colour in her cheeks. 'Am I over-dressed?' She looked at the other girl in her simple black dress, 'I thought when I saw you that perhaps I wasn't quite right . . . '

'Oh, don't worry. She didn't mean that. Besides,' she did a little pirouette, 'all this simplicity is deceptive. These dresses cost a bomb. You know they're made specially for us, designed by Nils Piersen.'

But before Cindy had time to register surprise that the well known couturier was prepared to take on such apparently trifling tasks, she saw Mr Gascoigne bustling towards the entrance. All evidence of nervous tension was forgotten, his benevolent smile fixed firmly in position as if the last thing he were thinking of was business, the sordid affair of making money.

And then, the showroom appeared to Cindy's bewildered gaze to be filled with dozens of robed figures, all chattering at the tops of their voices, all gesticulating as if their words were inadequate for what they wished to convey. In fact, if she had troubled to count, Cindy would have discovered that there were no more than a dozen and four of these seemed content to sit in chairs by the door and let the others do all the negotiating.

Immediately, Marjorie, Miss Cavendish and Mr Debenham were fully occupied with their task of showing the customers what they wished to see. From her position in one corner of the room, Cindy saw the brilliant flash of diamonds, the fiery riot of precious stones and the softer, subtler gleam of rich metals. The breath-taking impression was intensified, magnified and duplicated a hundred times by the gleam of the crystal chandeliers, by the reflections of the mirrored walls.

Through one of these mirrors, she saw Mr Gascoigne disappear, followed by a tall figure dressed in pure white robes. A moment later, the almost silent whine of the lift told her that Mr Gascoigne had gone upstairs to his office to talk more confidentially to his customer.

Cindy sighed and leaned lightly against an ornamental marble pillar. Her feet in the high-heeled boots were beginning to ache. It had been a long day and after the excitement and anticipation of the last few hours, there was a sense of anti-climax. She wished she were in Marjorie's shoes, doing something instead of just standing here feeling like an ornament.

As if by some kind of telepathy, she

heard Marjorie's voice call over to her. 'Miss Charles.' Her tone was cool and business-like and quite different from the one she had been using a short time before.

'Yes, Miss Smith?' Entering into the spirit of the business world Cindy levered herself away from her ornamental pose and stepped across to the counter.

'Would you look after the Sheikha.' The word tripped easily from Marjorie's lips as she turned to look meaningfully at Cindy. 'I just want to go to the strong-room to fetch some more bracelets.' She turned back to the customer. 'Miss Charles will tell you anything you want to know,' she said sweetly then with another smile she walked to the back of the shop.

Cindy had a moment's panic when the trays of jewelled bangles seemed to swim and merge in front of her eyes. But almost at once her own good sense re-asserted itself. It wasn't as if she was expected to sell anything. She was really just keeping an eye on the merchandise, and besides Marjorie would be back in a minute. She smiled and reached out a hand to hold up for examination a particularly ornate piece.

'You like this one?' The voice, light and amusing, sounding totally English brought the girl's eyes up for the first time to look at her customer. She had been aware of enveloping silks in a subtle shade of saffron, of a musky exotic scent and she had even noticed vaguely the small hands, pale unlined and with pinkly varnished finger-nails. And of course adorned with several valuable looking rings.

'I beg your pardon?' Cindy looked at the smiling face which was older than she would have judged by the voice and hands. But although she was no longer young, the Sheikha's beauty was scarcely dimmed. Her eyes were dark, almond shaped and set in the pale skin of a small heart-shaped face. The narrow nose, slightly aquiline could give the features in repose the appearance of patrician haughtiness but at the moment there was no mistaking the friendly look on the woman's face. Cindy found her lips curving into an answering smile.

'I asked if this is the one you like?' She took the bracelet heavily wrought in white gold with a diamond clasp, moving it so that the overhead lights caught the jewels and made them glitter.

'Yes,' Cindy was more than willing to help with her advice. 'It is a beautiful piece and the workmanship is excellent.' She put her head to one side and eyed it appraisingly. 'And the diamonds are very fine.' When she saw the Sheikha purse her lips and look amused, Cindy stopped speaking, realising that she was sounding rather pompous.

Apparently losing interest in the girl's opinion, the woman put the bracelet down on the counter, a little apart from the other bracelets, applying herself once more to making her choice. Then before any more was said, Marjorie came back from the strongroom, placed several boxes on the glass top and began to open them, showing the contents to the customer.

Feeling herself in the way, Cindy drifted away from the counter and back to her position on the outskirts of the activity. With difficulty she stifled a yawn. For all the good she was doing here she might as well have been at home. There was a particular pro-gramme on television she had wanted to see. Now she was bound to miss it.

She looked up as she heard the soft thud of the lift gently coming to a halt and an instant later, the door at the far side opened and Mr Gascoigne fol-lowed by the tall Arab came back into the room. She saw her employer look towards her, sensed that he was about to put up a hand to attract her attention. At that very moment, how-ever, Miss Cavendish came up to him, spoke and then led him over to the other side of the room where she was dealing with two men and a woman. The Arab who had come down with Mr Gascoigne seemed to be intensely interested in a display of antique silver in one of the showcases and then he went over to speak to one of the men who had remained sitting by the door.

Cindy's suspicion that these were servants were confirmed by the manner of the man who rose to answer some question that had been put to him. While there was nothing obsequious in his appearance there was a hint of deference that indicated he was not dealing with someone of his own rank. She watched him sit down again when the man in white turned away.

Then before she had time to form any more impressions, Mr Gascoigne had come across to her and was asking her to go upstairs and fetch her sketches. He was in a mood of excessive good-humour.

'I have been telling the Sheikh all about you, my dear. Said that if it was modern designs he was after, then he need look no further.' He glanced across the room to where the man was once more involved with his friends, 'He's a strange man. I wonder . . . ' He pulled himself up. 'But I mustn't keep you back. Hurry along, Cindy.'

It took her no more than a few minutes to go upstairs to her workroom and take from the top drawer of her desk the pile of sketches she had prepared before leaving that afternoon. She opened the blue folder to check them briefly and then went back downstairs in the lift.

She was amazed when she opened the door into the showroom to hear the noise that such a small number of people was capable of making. It sounded, she thought just like the tower of Babel but here they were speaking only two languages, English and presumably Arabic. She swiftly crossed the room to where Mr Gascoigne was surveying the scene with some complacency.

'The sketches, sir.' She held the folder out to him.

'What? Oh, yes. I'll just get the Sheikh. He'll probably want to have a word with you.' And he turned away.

Rather than stand in the centre of the floor, Cindy was drawn back to where Marjorie seemed to be completing her business with the Sheikha. It was apparent from the salesgirl's expression that she was more than happy with the outcome. She made up several parcels which she handed across the counter and then swept up all the remaining stock which had to be returned to the strong-room. Her look of appeal sent Cindy over to entertain the customer.

'You have found what you want?' It was the only thing she could think of saying as Marjorie hurried away.

'Yes, thank you.' The woman pulled part of her saffron silk robe across her head and proceeded to put the packages away in her crocodile hand-bag. All except one flat narrow package. 'I think I have everything now.' She paused and her dark eyes looked steadily at the girl. 'But this is for you.'

Her small hand came out and pushed the package across the glass top.

'For me?' Cindy smiled, convinced that she had misheard.

'For you.' A smile touched the carmined mouth. 'You sound refreshingly surprised.'

'But what is it?' Still Cindy made no move to pick up the package from the counter.

A tinkling laugh sounded in the girl's ears. 'Oh . . . It is the bracelet which you admired.'

Again Cindy thought she hadn't heard properly. And then when it dawned on her that the woman was perfectly serious, she felt the blood pounding in her ears. Instinctively she took a step backwards, away from the counter.

'I — I,' she stammered, 'I couldn't possibly.' She tried to imagine just how much a bracelet of that quality might cost. She tried and failed. 'No. I couldn't possibly.'

The woman laughed again, a sound of pure amusement and a sound which attracted attention despite the loud murmur of other voices. From the corner of her eye, Cindy saw Mr Gascoigne bear down on them. Mr Gascoigne and the tall man, the one who was supposed to be interested in her sketches. Miserably aware of the colour mounting in her cheeks, she wondered if she had been guilty of some grave solecism, if the refusal of a gift was considered a great insult in Middle Eastern cultures.

She knew that Mr Gascoigne was looking questioningly from the Sheikha to herself but she refused to meet his enquiring glance. Meanwhile the other man listened to an incomprehensible torrent of Arabic from the woman, replied calmly in a deep mellow voice before turning for the first time to look at the girl who stood on the other side of the glass counter.

Unwillingly, resentfully even, Cindy raised her face to his, furious with the circumstances which had made her so conspicuous. But when she looked at him closely for the first time, the shock was so great that it almost drove the breath from her body.

At a distance she had taken note of his height, the small dark beard. She had even admitted to herself that the long robes emphasised rather than detracted from his obvious masculinity, conveyed an air of mystery and romance which could not fail to attract the least vulnerable female.

And now! Here was a man looking like an Arab, talking like an Arab, dressing and behaving like one. And yet his eyes were the greenest she had ever seen in her life. Her heart gave a quite unexpected somersault. She had never imagined, not in her wildest flights of fancy, that Arabs could have green eyes.

Then, as if his attention had been caught by her agitation, she realised that her scrutiny was being returned. The casual appraising look he had been prepared to spare her narrowed, intensified and gave way to something more intimate which flared briefly between them.

2

For what seemed an age, their eyes locked, all the noise of the surrounding chatter faded into the distance. Neither was aware that the Sheikha, standing so close to them, looked from one to the other, first in surprise, then with an almost imperceptible change of expression.

At last, something forced itself on Cindy's consciousness, something intruded upon this delicious euphoric floating sensation that caused her to wrench her gaze from the mesmeric green one and to look with unseeing eyes to the petite figure by his side. Not that the Sheikha was paying any attention to the girl behind the counter. Of course she wasn't. She was laughing up into the face of the man, speaking volubly and gesturing eloquently with the small delicate hands.

Cindy, for no reason that was sensible, felt deliberately snubbed and tried to hide the colour mounting in her cheeks by bending down to fiddle with the sliding door at the back of the counter. Her cheeks burned when she heard the woman's soft laughter followed by the deep tones in which amusement was so overt. But she couldn't remain bent over the cabinet for ever and she straightened up feeling awkward and foolish.

'My mother . . . ' His accent was pure English public school. Her eyes shot up to his, fascinated to see if perhaps she had made a mistake. She hadn't. 'My mother would like you to have this.'

Cindy, unable to cope with the tumult of excitement that his gaze caused, looked down at the hand touching the narrow parcel. She noticed the long fingers, the short well-shaped nails, her eyes travelled to the wrist where the dark hairs showed beneath the bracelet of the heavy gold watch

before disappearing inside the loose
flowing sleeve of his robe. She realised
that he was expecting an answer to
what he had said. Surely he had
mentioned his mother. She raised her
eyes to the woman's.

'I cannot accept such a present. You
must realise . . . ' She sought for the
proper words to refuse, feeling that
whatever she said might cause offence.
'It is not the custom in this country.' As
she spoke these words she felt rather
pleased. Whatever their own customs,
they must respect those of their hosts.
She refused to look at the man who was
studying her so intently, appealing
instead to the woman who she felt
certain would be more likely to
understand.

His mother! That she would not have
guessed. It was possible of course that
she could be the mother of a man in his
thirties; she had heard that Arab
women married very young. And there
was a certain resemblance of manner
more than appearance — they certainly

had the same highly-bred cast of features. But he was a giant of a man to be the product of the Sheikha. A glance in his direction confirmed all that she was thinking but awareness of his continued scrutiny brought a return of her confusion. A tremulous smile hovered over her lips as she turned again to the woman. Her eyes were on her son but she turned to Cindy with a smile and a sigh.

'Of course.' She looked away as if she suddenly found the entire business boring, speaking a few words in Arabic over her shoulder.

Cindy saw the relaxed lounging figure straighten up, the narrow package disappeared inside his robes and at last his riveted gaze released the girl. She gave a shuddering sigh which might have been relief and looked up gratefully as Mr Gascoigne, clearly bewildered by something, some underlying tension he couldn't understand, coughed discreetly and rustled the papers he was holding in his hands.

'Ah, Cindy . . . ' He cleared his throat, 'This is Sheikh Al Adham. I have been explaining about your work to him . . . '

Quite abruptly, the Sheikh looked pointedly at his watch. 'I think perhaps we have done enough for one evening. We could look at the sketches some other time.' Something in his tone suggested to Cindy that he had lost interest in her work and she felt vexation bring colour to her cheeks. And in a moment she was watching the backs of the other three as, without another glance in her direction, they went towards the door.

At once, as if at a pre-arranged signal, the others in the shop all drifted after them, the servants who had apparently been on guard getting up and going out ahead of the main party. She heard Mr Gascoigne bidding them goodnight, caught the murmur of the Sheikha's reply, saw the rather theatrical salaam given by one of the men. Then two enormously long black cars slid forward to the doors of the shop, the entire party disappeared into the vehicles and they glided silently away into the night.

★   ★   ★

Marjorie and Cindy decided to treat themselves to a meal on the way home. They had discovered that they lived fairly close to each other and it seemed sensible to share a taxi part of the way. Besides, Mr Gascoigne had been so pleased with the result of the evening that he had given each of them permission to claim for a meal from petty cash next day.

'I hope he doesn't forget.' Marjorie frowned over the menu in the small Italian restaurant. 'Because I intend to go the whole hog and have the Osso Bucco.' She grinned, showing her small white teeth. 'I've only had it once before. The first time Rick took me out and I thought he was better-off than he really is.'

'Rick, is he . . . '

'Yes.' Marjorie blushed a little, looking down at the table. 'We're getting engaged at Christmas.'

'Oh, Congratulations. Well, you should be all right for a ring at cost price!'

'Oh, yes. Old Gaskers isn't bad that way. But even at cost we won't be able to afford anything from the regular stock. Still, we'll be able to get something more modest at trade rates. By the way . . . ' She looked curiously at Cindy. 'Did I see you refusing a present from the Sheikha?'

Cindy laughed apologetically. 'Yes, it seemed slightly ridiculous. She offered me a bracelet.'

'And you didn't take it?' The other girl's voice showed lack of comprehension. 'You know we've all been given presents. At least, I think the others have as well.'

'What? Do you mean, it's usual for them to give presents in shops?'

'I don't know about other shops but it's common enough in jewellers.

Although I've never seen them offer anything quite as valuable as that bracelet before. Yes,' she went on casually, 'the firm will always take anything back. At a price of course. Some girls do quite well out of it.'

'And . . . ' Cindy hesitated. 'What did you get tonight?'

'Oh, tonight. I got a brooch. You noticed that I was showing those to the Sheikha earlier? I left it at the showroom and I'll get a credit tomorrow.'

'Oh,' Cindy felt slightly chilled by this attitude to gifts. 'I see.'

'Don't sound so disapproving, love. At the moment I'm more interested in bricks and mortar than in brooches. Can you blame me?'

'No, of course not.' Cindy laughed. 'I suppose I made the mistake of admiring the bracelet.'

'Oh, yes. She may have thought you were expecting a gift and that you were saying what you would like.'

'Do you think so?' Cindy was aghast

45

and one hand went involuntarily to her face. 'Oh, I should hate it if she thought so.'

'Well, I shouldn't worry about it.' Marjorie was comfortingly matter-of-fact. 'She couldn't have thought that for long if you refused it.' She leaned her chin in her hands and looked across the table at her companion. Her eyes were bright with interest. 'But what did you think of the man? Wasn't he a dream?'

'Which man?' Innocently Cindy returned the look, even managing to draw her brows together in a tiny frown. 'There were several there.'

'Oh, come off it!' Marjorie laughed in sheer disbelief. 'You know exactly which man.' She watched the colour run up under the other girl's skin. 'Yes, that one,' and she laughed again knowingly.

'Oh, him.' Cindy looked down and fiddled with her knife. 'What about him?'

'I just asked what you thought of him,' said Marjorie drily.

'He looks rather nice,' Cindy capitulated with a smile.

'Rather nice!' Marjorie teased. 'Well, if that's how you like to put it. I just thought he looked like everyone's Arab Sheikh rolled into one.' She sighed dramatically. 'It's just as well that I'm committed. Otherwise I might be in danger — Ah.' She broke off as the waiter came over flicking a cloth over the table. 'Yes, we're ready to order now.' And she picked up the menu, frowning with the concentration the menu in Italian deserved.

But later that night when she lay in bed, Cindy found it more difficult to pretend that the Sheikh had made very little impression on her. To be truthful she could think of nothing else but that shattering moment when casually, without realising the importance of the encounter she looked up into his eyes. As she relived the incident she felt a wave of intense, passionate longing sweep through her causing her to blush even in the darkness.

Then immediately she laughed and gave herself a little mental shake. Don't be a fool, Cindy, she admonished severely. You're acting like a seventeen-year-old instead of twenty-two, like the heroine of some improbable romance not a semi-successful career girl. In any case even if he weren't an Arab, is it likely that he would have any real interest in a girl like you? Of course not, she answered herself. There's too much disparity in your positions, both social and financial. He's probably used to having any girl he fancies. Not your type at all, my dear. Best to think of him as the glamorous star whom you sometimes see when you go to the cinema. Nice to dream about but essentially a fantasy figure. And having thus spoken to herself firmly, she went to sleep at last, her face wet with tears.

It was a week before she began to settle down to work again, before she was able to make a determined effort to push thoughts of him to the back of her mind. In that week, she and Marjorie, realised that with a little rearranging they could make their lunch breaks coincide and now took their snack meals together in a little café just round the corner from the showroom.

An almost instant rapport sprang up between the girls so that Cindy, who was normally reticent by nature found herself satisfying the other girl's curiosity without any of the reserve with which she would have parried anyone else's questioning.

'But you can't tell me,' Marjorie stated on one of these occasions, 'You can't tell me that you haven't had plenty of boyfriends. Not a girl like you.'

'A girl like me?' Cindy laughed and wrinkled her nose. 'That might mean anything.'

'You know well enough what I mean,' Marjorie took a bite out of a huge cream bun. 'So . . . ' the tip of a small pink tongue came out to chase a minute piece of jam which had escaped. ' . . . I'm not going to make you any more conceited by explaining.'

'Oh, another compliment?' Cindy teased. 'More conceited. Ouch.'

'Sorry. Oh . . . You know what I mean.'

'I don't.' Cindy was primly aggravating, then relenting, 'Oh, of course I'm not going to tell you that I haven't had boyfriends if that was your original question. I've almost forgotten.'

'But no one special?' Marjorie had finished her bun and now stirred her coffee thoughtfully.

'No. Not really.' Cindy sighed. 'In fact not at all.'

'But what about all those dishy young men at Art College? I would have thought they'd be queueing up to paint you.'

There was a faint giggle from Cindy. 'I don't know that I'd have wanted any of them to paint me. Most of them were inclined to the surrealistic school and I doubt if I would have been flattered by proof of how they saw me.'

Marjorie grinned and reached for her bag. 'I see what you mean. I've never been very keen on that kind of thing myself.' She got up, hitching her handbag over one shoulder. 'Shall we go?' She led the way through the crowded restaurant and out into the mid-day bustle of Oxford Street. 'Oh, well,' she continued the conversation as they walked along, looking into the windows of the fashion houses, 'I suppose one of these days it will simply happen. Hm, I like that.' She pointed to some material draped over a spinning-wheel in one of the displays. 'I could make a nice skirt and bolero with a yard and a half. But perhaps not . . . ' She dragged Cindy away as if she was being encouraged into wild indulgence. 'I'm trying to save, after all. Yes,' she walked on firmly, 'one of these days, you'll just meet someone and that will be it.' Her sigh was one of deep contentment. 'Just like Rick and me.'

Hastily trying to dispel thoughts of green eyes and dazzling robes, Cindy encouraged her friend to talk. 'It was like that, was it? Just like in books?'

'Yes. Yes, it was.' The colour rose a little in Marjorie's cheeks as she turned to look at Cindy. 'I can see that you're smiling but just you wait. When you begin to look all moony, I'll remind you about your cynical attitude.'

'Well, I shan't mind.' Cindy laughed aloud. 'Only . . . I'm fairly sure that you won't have the chance. Now,' she glanced at her watch, 'we'd better be thinking about going back. I don't want old Gaskers to be making pointed remarks about prolonged lunch hours. Or, even worse, to have Miss Grange looking pointedly at her clock.'

'Oh, her! She's just jealous.'

'Jealous? Why should she be jealous?'

'No reason. Except to someone as tied up in knots as she is. But like I told you before, you're the only one the boss calls by her first name. And when you are the private secretary, then these things can hurt.' She finished with a not unsuccessful parody of Miss Grange's slightly mincing tones.

'Marjorie.' It was a voice of laughing remonstrance. 'But . . . Do you think she fancies Mr Gascoigne? She can't. Can she?'

'Well, as I said, there's no accounting for who or what Miss Grange fancies. I think that beneath that rather prim exterior beats a fiery maidenly heart. In short, I can imagine she might be a fairly sexy piece.'

So, when Cindy rushing upstairs to her workroom, conscious of being two minutes late encountered Miss Grange at the top of the stairs, she felt guilty and embarrassed over the way they had analysed the woman's private feelings.

'Oh, Miss Grange. Hello.'

But the secretary didn't reply to her greeting. Instead she gave the impression of being censorious about Cindy being late and also let her eyes rest disapprovingly on the girl's flushed cheeks and the curls of hair which had escaped from the wide restraining band. Then she spoke.

'Mr Gascoigne would like to see you

at once. It is quite five minutes since he asked me to call you in to his office. I was forced to tell him that you hadn't returned from lunch. I suggest you tidy your hair before you go in.' She turned away. 'A few minutes more won't matter now.'

As she watched the figure in the smart but severe brown dress walk away from her in the direction of Mr Gascoigne's office, Cindy felt indignation boil up within her. She felt furious with herself for failing to point out that it had only just gone one-thirty when she was supposed to return from lunch but more incensed to think that Miss Grange was capable of telling all sorts of tales about her to the boss.

She flung away in the direction of the cloakroom and while she was savagely combing out her long hair, it gave her great satisfaction to imagine that it was Miss Grange's hair she was brushing, that she had loosened that neat prim little knot at the back and that she was using the same hard painful strokes

. . . Suddenly Cindy smiled at herself, half in genuine amusement, half in irritated frustration. She'd better get a move on or the boss would begin to think that she *was* taking extended lunch breaks.

'You wanted to see me, Mr Gascoigne?' There had been no exchange of glances as she had walked through the secretary's sanctum but Cindy had seen the woman's finger flick the switch, heard her voice murmur as she reached the great mahogany door.

'Come in, Cindy. Come in.' As usual he was sitting behind the heavy wooden desk, his blotter immaculate on the tooled leather top, the silver and gold pens laid in order on the crystal tray. She supposed that he did work sometimes but all the evidence she saw of such a thing was the pile of letters that Miss Grange sometimes pushed in front of him for his signature. She waited, standing rather awkwardly in front of the desk, until his next words percolated through her daydream. Obediently, she sat down.

'Well, Cindy. And how are you? Still hearing from your mother, I hope?'

'I had a letter this morning. She seems to be well, Mr Gascoigne.'

'Nevertheless you must miss her. I thought it was a pity when I heard that she was going to re-marry. An American. If it had been an Englishman, then you would still have had a home . . . '

Cindy, still self-conscious about her mother's sudden decision to re-marry, at once sprang to her defence. 'Oh, I don't mind. After all, I had been away from home for so long, since I was fourteen. I went to boarding school when my father died, you know. With mother having to travel the world so much, it seemed the sensible thing. And I was very pleased when she married Charles.' The lie had been repeated so often that it scarcely seemed like a falsehood any longer.

'Well, I'm glad. And I suppose one of these days you'll be going off to America?'

'No. At least, not to live. Of course I'll be going out on holiday whenever I want to. But I shan't live anywhere but in England.'

'Good. Good.' Like most people, Mr Gascoigne liked to have his own prejudices confirmed by others and Cindy's remarks assured him that he was right in thinking that England was the only place in the world where one should live. He had an even more severe chauvanism that made him pity those who lived as far north as Bedford.

'Well, my dear, this is very nice but of course it isn't why I asked you to come along this afternoon . . . ' He paused and Cindy was forced to say something which would fill the space about them.

'Of course not, Mr Gascoigne.'

'No. I have a rather nice little job for you this afternoon.' He beamed across at her. 'I'm sorry I couldn't give you any more warning but I just got the phone call when you were out at lunch.'

Cindy wondered if she ought to apologise for being late but on the whole she thought not. Never explain, never apologise, one of the college lecturers used to say. And although normally Cindy didn't see any reason behind the saying, this was one of the times when she accepted the dictum without question.

'Oh . . . ' It seemed a nice compromise.

'Yes. I want you to go round to the Hilton Hotel and take all your sketches with you. The ones we spoke about, from the Nefertiti collection.'

'My sketches?' Still she wasn't sure what he meant but she didn't like the trembling feeling of excitement in her stomach.

'Yes, yes.' There was a hint of impatience in Mr Gascoigne's voice and he had forgotten that his explanation had been sketchy. He reached for the gold pen furthest from him on the tray. 'The Sheikha rang when you were out. I told her you would be there as soon as possible. Now go along, my dear, but come to me with your sketches before you leave. I want to make certain that you understand exactly . . . '

Without knowing how she got there, Cindy found herself standing outside the door, leaning back against its heavy panels as if for support. Now she had no inclination to plan retribution on Miss Grange. All she could think of now was the awful feeling in her inside, as if she had just come down in a lift at twenty miles an hour. And had left her stomach behind.

3

By the time she had reached the foyer of the hotel, Cindy had her feelings under some sort of control so that she was able to walk across the busy foyer to the reception desk with an admirable air of coolness. How often she had driven down Park Lane, had looked into the softly lighted interior from the upper deck of a bus without imagining that she would soon be speaking to the young man behind the desk . . .

'The Sheikha Al Adham?' He answered her enquiry. 'Certainly, if you would just care to take a seat for a moment.'

Dismissed, she turned away, suddenly feeling lost in the midst of this expensive jewelled, scented crowd, her folder of sketches clutched firmly under one arm. She wished she might have had time to go back to the flat to put on something different but Mr Gascoigne had insisted there was no time for that and had assured her that her navy velvet trouser suit would be perfectly adequate.

'Miss Charles?' She turned swiftly at the sound of her name to see the small page boy addressing her. 'The Sheikha will see you now. If you care to follow me.'

The trip upwards was almost silent and as she followed the small figure along the corridor the only sound she could hear was the frantic hammer of her own pulses. Then she was being shown into a large sitting-room and the door had closed behind her. The sense of anti-climax was overwhelming when she realised that the room was empty — but after a moment, the door through which she herself had come opened, and Sheikha Al Adham came inside.

'Ah, Miss Charles, is it not?' The Sheikha waved a hand towards one of the seats. 'Please sit down.'

Rather awkwardly, Cindy found herself sitting on the edge of the seat only too well aware that she was being scrutinised very closely indeed by the Sheikha. As the older woman showed no sign of speaking the girl felt obliged to say something.

'Mr Gascoigne said you wanted to see the sketches.'

'Yes. I see you have brought them.' Her eyes rested briefly on the folder which Cindy had put down on the table in front of her before returning to the girl's face. 'But first you would like some tea.'

It seemed not to be a question and Cindy heard herself murmuring some incoherent acceptance.

'I have already asked them to bring it up.' The woman sat on a chair opposite Cindy and reached with one of her small delicate hands towards the cigarette box on the nearby table. 'Do you smoke, Miss Gordon?'

'No, I don't, thank you.' Cindy watched with concealed curiosity as the woman selected a long black cigarette, placed it in a silver holder and lit it. The air with which she leaned back in the chair drawing the smoke deep inside her lungs with obvious satisfaction was just a little incongruous with the enveloping Arab garments she wore and Cindy bowed her head to hide the twitching of her mouth.

'You are wise.' The dark eyes had missed nothing of her amusement and sparkled in sympathy. 'Not to smoke, I mean. I ought not to smoke so many. My son is always telling me so.'

At the reference to the man who had occupied her thoughts so much Cindy felt the quick colour rise in her cheeks but the Sheikha went on as if she had not noticed. 'And I can see you think it strange. Such evidence of a different life . . . ' she held up some of her voluminous garment ruefully, ' . . . and this.' She waved the cigarette. 'But Arab women have found consolation in nicotine for many generations. I'm sure my great-grandmother smoked when it would have been considered very fast for an English woman to do so. Ah, here comes the tea.' She looked round at the sound, the very gentle sound of crockery being rattled before a maid came into the room with a tray.

While they drank tea and ate the luscious cakes which had arrived with it, Cindy found she was being gently quizzed about herself. She explained that she lived in a tiny flat, that her mother had gone to live in New York and that she had been working for Daubeny and Gascoigne for only about six months.

'But . . . ' The Sheikha put down her cup and lit another cigarette, ' . . . Mr Gascoigne tells me that you won the gold medal at your Art College.'

'Yes.'

'I suspect that is why you are working for them. Although he doesn't give that impression, I'm sure Mr Gascoigne is a very shrewd businessman. Now,' she left her seat and sat down beside the girl on the sofa, 'if I can look at your work . . . '

They sat for more than an hour looking at the sketches which Cindy had brought with her. They were mainly from the new collection she had been working or since she had joined the firm and which Mr Gascoigne had christened the Nefertiti, reference to ancient Egyptian designs which had inspired the work. Although she could not say what gave her the impression, Cindy thought that the Sheikha was less than enthusiastic about what she had been shown. Her suspicions were confirmed when, after they had gone through the folder several times, Cindy with a pencil at the ready, pointing out the various intricities of the design, the woman sighed and then shook her head.

'I am sorry, Miss Charles.' And there was a genuine regret in her sympathetic eyes. 'Perhaps I ought to have known. Mr Gascoigne did mention Nefertiti and that should have given me some indication about the trend of your work.'

'You don't like it.' Cindy felt sick with disappointment.

'I like them. Of course I do. But I really wanted something different. For a young girl, you understand. These . . . ' she laid a hand on the folder, 'these are too sophisticated. For a woman in her thirties, I should say. I thought of something,' she hesitated, 'something more like that pendant you were wearing that evening when we came to the showroom. And the earrings.'

'Oh, those?' Cindy stared in disbelief. 'But they were cheap little things. I designed the set when I was at College and it cost very little to make. I didn't think you wanted . . . '

'Oh, make no mistake, we want something special. No, what I meant was that I liked the style of the thing you were wearing. It is just the kind of thing I had in mind.'

'Well . . . If that is what you want there would be no trouble. I could soon do some sketches.'

'Could you? You see, my niece, my adopted niece is being married and I want to make her a really beautiful gift, something original just for her. Something that a young girl would like to *wear*, not just an investment for the future.'

'Yes, I see.'

'Then you will do it.' The Sheikha rose, glancing at the jewelled watch on her wrist. 'I am so pleased. And now I must hurry. I am meeting my son downstairs at five. You will excuse me?' She opened the door and walked through the hall with the girl. 'I shall hear from Mr Gascoigne. Goodbye, Miss Charles.'

In a moment Cindy found herself down in the foyer again. It was too late to go back to work so she looked round for a telephone to call Mr Gascoigne whom she knew would still be in his office. When she had spoken to him, reporting the result of her interview with the Sheikha, Cindy paused a moment to adjust her folder of sketches before going through the huge swing doors and into the street.

But just then, as she stood back against the wall, there was a considerable bustle at the doors and a large party of Arabs came through the foyer. Heads were turned as the group walked slowly across the floor, the men absorbed in the conversation they were having. But it was at one man in particular Cindy was looking. He was taller than the others, none of whom was short, and his tallness seemed to attract every eye in the room. She watched the animation with which he spoke to his companions, saw a flash of teeth as he suddenly laughed, then a moment later, she saw him stride across towards the lifts, his white robe floating out about him, an air of impatience in the set of his shoulders.

She allowed herself to sink down on to a convenient chair. Even at that distance, even although he hadn't glanced in her direction, she was aware of his magnetism. She gave a shuddering little sigh and raised her chin. And a quick glance round the room told her that possibly every other female in the room had the same feelings as herself. Quite simply, he was the kind of man women would always be aware of.

By the time a week had passed, Cindy once again began to think that she had had her last contact with the Al Adham family. And to be quite truthful, she assured herself insincerely, it was probably all for the best. There was no doubt but that she regretted the Sheikha's reaction to her sketches, it would have been a feather in her cap to have clinched a big order, but someone else would come along who would love the Nefertiti range; in her bones she knew that they were good.

But if she were to keep her feet on the ground, then it was perhaps as well that she shouldn't come in contact with such exotic acquaintances, even on a strictly business footing. Having made up her mind on this point, it was difficult to explain why she was giving so much of her time, both at work and back at her flat in the evenings, to the designing of a completely new range of jewellery. Privately she had christened it the Trysting range but of course her choice of name had nothing at all to do with anything that the Sheikha had said to her at their last meeting.

Much of her spare time was being spent with Marjorie and at last she allowed the older girl to persuade her to make up a foursome with herself, Rick and a friend he was intending to bring up with him for the weekend.

'Oh, all right.' Cindy uncurled herself from the sofa and went to turn over the record on her small player. 'But I would have thought that you and Rick would be more anxious to be on your own than with other people.'

'Well, I want you to meet him.' Marjorie kept her eyes fixed on the tablecloth she was embroidering. 'I have a reason for that.' she added mysteriously.

'Oh?' Cindy, invo[l]
culties with a tem[...]
scarcely understood [...]
ion was saying. 'We [...]
once. Just for you.' [...]
kneeling position [...]
fireplace. 'I've ne[...]
for blind dates.' [...]

miss the c[...]
tomorrow [...]
arranged [...]
'Jamie [...]
'C [...]
th[...]

'Not since I got caught when [...]
college. Someone persuaded me to
meet this medical student. Then when
we arrived at the dance where we were
all meeting up, Derek turned out to be
a whole head shorter than I am. I think
he felt worse about it than I did.'

'You needn't worry about that.'
Marjorie bit through a piece of
embroidery silk with her small white
teeth. 'Jamie is at least six feet tall.
Rather like a Norse God in fact.'

'I bet.' There was a snort of derision
from Cindy. 'I haven't seen many of
those about.'

'True.' Marjorie wasn't the least bit
put out by her friend's scepticism.
'That's why you would be foolish to

71

ance. So, when I ring
ght, I'll tell Rick that it's all
for Saturday.' She paused.
s being our Best Man.'
?' Cindy's head shot up. 'Does
mean you've fixed a date for the
edding?'

'We'd like to. But it will depend on whether Rick manages to get a move back to Head Office. I don't particularly want to give up my job at Gascoigne's just yet. We really need the money for a year or two. It's a pity . . .' Her voice trailed away.

'What? That you're getting married?' Cindy teased.

'No, of course not. I was just thinking, it's a pity you and I didn't get to know each other before. It would have been nice if we could have shared a flat. And much cheaper.'

'Yes,' Cindy replied carefully. Fond as she was of the other girl, she didn't want to share a flat with anyone. 'But yours isn't much bigger than this.' She waved a hand round disparagingly. 'It would be much too cramped with two.'

'But we might have got a bigger one.'

'Yes, but that would have cost more and would have been just as expensive.'

'Well, perhaps you're right. It maybe wouldn't have been such a good idea.' Marjorie sighed and began to fold up her sewing. 'Anyway it's too late to worry about that now.' She yawned loudly. 'I suppose I'd better make tracks for home, love.' She showed no immediate signs of doing so. 'Where would you like to go on Saturday? Shall we just make it Genarro's or there's that little Greek place in the basement. On Saturday nights they sometimes push the tables closer so that there's room to dance.'

'I don't mind.' Cindy looked at her friend. 'But maybe we'd better forget the dancing. Just in case you haven't told me the truth about Jamie. I don't want any repetition of what happened with Derek.'

But as it happened, they had to change their plans for Saturday for by the end of the week, events in Cindy's life had taken a very different and unexpected turn.

'Mr Gascoigne would like to see you at once, Miss Charles.'

'Thank you, Miss Grange.' Cindy had decided that it was best to treat her colleague with the formality which she showed but she still sighed when the door closed without another word from the woman. How much nicer it would have been if the atmosphere upstairs had been more friendly. She folded away her work and then walked along the corridor to Mr Gascoigne's room.

'Ah, Cindy, my dear.' Her employer seemed in great good humour as he rose and came over the wide carpet to greet her. 'Sit down.' He held out a hand towards the chair in front of his desk and then seated himself on the edge of it, smiling down indulgently at the girl. 'You look very well, my dear.'

She smiled, not quite knowing how to answer such a remark and waited for him to go on. It took him a few moments, moments which he spent in reflection, his light blue eyes fixed so firmly on her that she edged uneasily on her chair.

'Ah yes, you must be wondering. Well . . . ' He eased himself away from his desk and round to his usual seat at the back. He beamed across at her. 'Tell me, Cindy, how long is it since you went abroad?'

'Abroad? Well, it must be two years. Mother and I went to France the summer before last.'

'France? I see. And what about your passport? Is that in order? And more important, it is a proper passport, I hope? Not just one of these Common Market jobs?'

'No, it's proper one. I thought that I might be going over to the States to see Mother . . . '

'Of course. Well, that's a good thing. Not that it would have been an insuperable difficulty. But still it will be one less thing to deal with at the last minute. Now . . . what else is there to think about?' Mr Gascoigne appeared to be in no hurry to come to the point of the summons to his office. 'Well, of course you'll want time off to go and buy some new clothes.' He glanced over in Cindy's direction. 'That shouldn't present any problems. And of course as you live on your own, you won't need to ask anyone's permission.' He smiled suddenly. 'No young men in the background who might raise objections, Cindy? That's one good thing. I wouldn't have liked to have to try to persuade a young husband to allow his wife to go out among all those handsome Arabs.'

Cindy felt the room begin to sway gently in front of her eyes while the face of her employer remained a smiling constant. The sensation lasted only a moment, then she at last found her voice. 'Do you mean Mr Gascoigne, that you want me . . . you would like me to go . . . abroad?'

Mr Gascoigne blinked comically. 'But didn't Miss Grange tell you so? I asked her to do so.' He frowned slightly. 'She may have misunderstood. Of course. She must have.' He laughed. 'You must have wondered just what I was talking about. But yes. That is exactly what I want you to do. I had a telephone call from the Sheikha this morning and it is all arranged. You are to leave for Saudi Arabia on Saturday morning.'

4

Cindy was thwarted in her first inclination towards refusal by the arrival of Miss Grange who appeared with some papers which Mr Gascoigne 'had required urgently'. In reply to his mild query about the misunderstanding she assured him that as she had been about to explain to Miss Charles that she might be asked to go to Arabia, her telephone had rung and she had merely hurried to answer it.

As she gave this assurance which their employer appeared to have no hesitation in accepting, she glanced sideways at Cindy as if challenging her to refute the claim. And although she was certain that Miss Grange had had no intention of putting her in the picture, Cindy found that her first idea of declining the suggestion that she should go to Saudi Arabia quickly ebbed. In fact, she felt that by accepting with an enthusiasm she didn't feel, somehow she was getting back at Miss Grange for all the months of unfriendliness.

Whatever her reasons, when she was whisked home by taxi that night, in something of a daze, she found that she was totally committed to the proposition that she should travel out to Saudi Arabia with the Sheikha at the end of the week.

The next few days went by in a bewildering whirl of shopping, the checking of travel documents, arranging for the required inoculations and finally, seeing her landlord to let him know that her flat would be unoccupied for the next week or two.

It was Friday night before she had time to do more than draw breath and she regretted that she had allowed Marjorie to persuade her to bring their date forward one day.

'It will be easy, love,' her friend had said the other day. 'They were coming down on the Friday in any case. Now they'll just have to hurry a bit more. No stopping at a pub on the way. And if you don't want to make it a long do, then we can just go and have a meal and then leave.'

'Well, certainly I don't want to be late. I've to be at the airport at ten so I'll be up with the lark.'

'Oh, you won't have any problem. And you've done all your packing, haven't you? All those lovely new clothes.' She sighed. 'I wish it was me. Even if I had to leave Rick for a few weeks, it would be worth it. I've always felt the desert must be the most romantic place.'

'I don't know. From what I've been reading in that book Mr Gascoigne lent me Riyadh isn't just as wonderful as you might think. And I don't suppose I'll see much of the desert. After all I'm going out there to work, you know.'

'So you keep telling me. But I can't see that designing a few pieces of jewellery for someone is going to be all that much of a task.'

'Oh, don't you? That's all you know about it. Ideas don't always just spring into the head, you know. In fact, I've an awful feeling that I might go out there and find that my mind has gone completely blank.'

'You'll be O.K. Aren't you taking that huge folio of designs that I saw coming down from the workroom today?'

'Yes. A lot of those are ones I did when I was at College. I hope I'll get some inspiration from them.'

'And the Sheikha? You're seeing her at the airport?'

'Yes. So I understand. I did hope that perhaps I might have been able to speak to her before we left. But I suppose she's busy.'

'Sure to be. Anyway, I'm glad you've agreed about Friday.' Marjorie wrinkled her nose and pretended that she hadn't heard her friend's little protest. 'It will do you good to have a night off before you go. And who knows,' she sighed and held out her hands in a pleading gesture, 'You might never come back. You might be whisked off on the back of an Arab steed.'

'I think the chances of that are extremely remote.' Cindy turned away so that her rising colour was hidden from Marjorie's tormenting gaze. 'From what you've said you're much more the romantic type than I am.'

'Don't be too sure of that. Anyway,' she abandoned her teasing manner and sat down on the rug, stretching her hands out to the gas fire. 'You will try to like Jamie, won't you? I told you that he was going to be best man. And,' her fingers pleated the soft folds of her dress, 'I would be really delighted, Cindy, if you would be my bridesmaid.'

And on the whole, decided Cindy, as she drove out to the airport next morning, she had liked Jamie very much indeed. He had been as tall as Marjorie had promised. And fair. But there his resemblance to a Norse God had begun and ended. Unless, she thought with a little giggle, Norse Gods had rather snub noses and the slightly tiresome habit of ending each sentence with the words, 'you know'.

That he had found Cindy more than a little to his liking was fairly obvious, so obvious in fact that Marjorie had kept sending little encouraging glances in Cindy's direction. However, it hadn't been too difficult to disengage herself from him at the end of the evening and she made up her mind that after the wedding was over they wouldn't have to see each other often.

So, it was more than a little surprising when she was standing about in the terminal building to feel an arm round her waist and a voice in her ear. 'All night I wondered if I had imagined how beautiful you were . . . ' Cindy raised startled brown eyes to the blue ones. ' . . . And, you know, I didn't imagine it at all.'

'Jamie! What on earth are you doing here?'

'I thought I had just explained. I wasn't going to let you go all that way without someone to see you off. Besides, I was determined to see you again as soon as possible. I'm not the kind to let the grass grow under my feet, you know.'

'Oh. I see.' Cindy spoke rather distractedly, for she had seen through the large area of plate glass that encircled the building, an important-looking group of black cars pull to a halt at the main entrance. Robed figures emerged and there was a flurry as they came inside the departure lounge.

Jamie, who had his back to the doors, grinned down at her and kept his hands linked about her slender waist. 'Come on, we'll go and have a cup of coffee. There's plenty of time, you know.'

'No.' Cindy dragged her attention back to her companion. 'This is where I was told to wait.' She gestured in the direction of the newspaper kiosk. 'I have my ticket and I checked in my luggage when I arrived but I think I'd better wait here.' She glanced back towards where she had seen the Arab party, disconcerted to find that they had disappeared. 'I really think you'd be as well to go, Jamie. Although it was so nice of you to come and see me off,' she relented.

'I shan't go until you've told me when you'll be back and exactly when I can take you out. Just the two of us. I can be quite persistent, you know.'

Cindy smiled, her heart warmed by his quite blatant admiration. 'I haven't booked my flight back yet. But I promise that whenever I get back to my flat I'll give you a ring.'

'That's a firm promise?' He looked as if he doubted her integrity somewhat. 'You won't forget?'

'I shan't forget. But now, I really would prefer you to go Jamie. I'm sure someone will be coming to meet me within a few minutes.'

'Well,' he said doubtfully, 'If that's what you really want. But,' she felt his hands tighten round her waist, felt the strength of his arms begin to pull her towards him, 'this is to help you remember that you made a promise.' And before she could do anything to escape, his mouth had come down on hers, one hand had moved to the back of her head so that he was impossible to avoid. It was an instant before she realised just what had happened, another before her indignation began to rise. She hated intimate behaviour in public and especially with someone whom she scarcely knew. She was about to pull herself violently away when she heard her name being spoken. The voice was as cold as chipped marble.

'Miss Charles.'

The sound, the cool, authoritative tone was effective in a way that Cindy's puny efforts would not have been. Jamie took his searching lips away from hers and released her abruptly. As she looked up into the disapproving face of the Sheikh Al Adham, Cindy felt the colour flood into her cheeks. 'Miss Charles.' He repeated.

'Yes.' She struggled to regain her

composure. 'I — this is Mr Woods,' she introduced Jamie. 'Sheikh Al Adham.'

Jamie murmured something but the Sheikh merely bowed his head rather brusquely, looked at the other man for a mere instant before turning his attention to Cindy. 'If you will come with me, Miss Charles.' The unusual green eyes betrayed nothing of his thoughts. 'We were unfortunately delayed and now it is necessary to board the plane as soon as possible. You have already checked in your luggage?'

'Yes.' Now that she had had a moment, Cindy was regaining her self-possession. She bent down for the bag that was at her feet. 'I am quite ready.'

As they walked across the hall, she was the merest step behind him, whether by his design or not, she was unable to decide. Her leave-taking of Jamie had been as brief as possible, with the tall white-robed figure hovering uncomfortably near. In fact, at that moment, Cindy was out of sympathy with the entire opposite sex. She was angry with Jamie, not only on her own account but more especially because he had happened to kiss her just at the wrong moment. And she was angry with the Sheikh for making her feel so guilty. After all, if there was one place where kissing might be allowed in public then surely it was the departure lounge of an international airport. And after all, this was England and not Saudi Arabia.

He swept on, Cindy in his wake hesitating briefly while she had her passport checked and then slowing his pace slightly as they walked down a long corridor.

'You are engaged to Mr Woods?' It was the first time he had spoken since they had left Jamie and his tone was quite mild, uninterested even as if he had been racking his brain for some suitable topic of conversation.

Relief made Cindy smile. 'Engaged? No, of course not. I met him for the first time last night.'

As she spoke she was looking at him, into those sea-green, jade-green eyes and as soon as the words were uttered she wished them back.

'I see.' There was a slight drawing together of the firmly marked eyebrows, a tightening of the mouth almost hidden by the small beard before he turned away through the automatic doors that led out to the great silver bird on the tarmac.

* * *

Dismay was Cindy's initial reaction when she climbed on board and found herself in a wholly alien company. That at least was a mistaken response for during the flight she was to discover that there were two more English nationals flying with them. But in the first class part of the aircraft, it seemed that Sheikh Al Adham and his family had taken over the entire section.

The first person she identified was the Sheikha who raised a hand and smiled when she caught sight of Cindy, motioning that she should go and sit beside her. Then her eyes moved to her son, following closely behind and she spoke a few words to him which Cindy did not understand.

He stood in front of them and gravely held out a hand to take her small case. There was a faint twinkle in his eyes as he looked at her, then, 'Forgive me Miss Charles. My mother has been reproving me for allowing you to carry your own baggage.' He swung it on to the rack above her head. 'I can only say that I forgot.' He smiled briefly and then went to sit somewhere behind them.

But that smile, faint though it had been, had set all Cindy's nerves quivering, she locked her hands together to stop their trembling and to help her retain her self-control. In fact, they were so firmly clasped together that the knuckles showed white. A fact that did not escape the notice of the Sheikha.

'You are nervous of flying, Miss Charles?'

'Nervous?' In surprise Cindy looked round, then seeing the Sheikha's eyes on her hands, she laughed ruefully and made a conscious effort to relax. 'No. I quite enjoy flying. I suppose I'm a little tense with all the hurry and excitement.' It did not seem the right moment to explain that her nervousness was almost entirely caused by the Sheikha's son.

'Ah, yes.' The Sheikha laughed. 'I'm sorry that you have been put to so much trouble. But I was so busy while I was in London that I was unable to see you again. In any case, I'm sure that it would be best for you to see Nevine before you design the jewellery for her.' She turned slightly in her seat so that she was looking directly at Cindy. 'And besides that, I hope that your visit to our country will be something which you will enjoy for its own sake.'

'I'm sure I shall.' Cindy spoke quietly, comforted by the woman's gentle friendliness. 'I think everyone has a longing to see the desert. And of course, I shall be looking all the time for 'inspiration'.' She spoke the last word self-mockingly and her mouth curved in a smile. 'It was always dinned into us at college that we must constantly keep our eyes open for ideas.'

'Then,' the dark eyes approved, 'we must see that we give your imagination plenty of time to work.'

The journey passed uneventfully although Cindy could not help noticing that the service and attention they received was much more lavish than she had been used to enjoying on her trips abroad. They had been airborne for less than an hour when the stewardesses brought round coffee, so strong and gritty that Cindy gasped when she raised the cup to her lips, and small sticky cakes. Surprisingly she found that once she had become used to the coffee, she liked its bitter flavour and found it refreshing.

She and the Sheikha were in the front row of seats in the section, behind them, several other Arab women to whom Cindy was introduced completed the immediate party and behind some flimsy curtains she understood the men were accommodated. As the journey progressed, the girl scarcely knew whether to be pleased or sorry that she had seen no more of the Sheikh. His mother appeared to have no complaints of the situation so Cindy assumed that this was their usual way of travelling.

The Sheikha indeed proved to be an interesting, amusing companion, showing none of the condescension that could possibly have been expected. Once or twice she mentioned her son but she said nothing about a husband so Cindy's curiosity on the matter was unsatisfied. During lunch, which was served with the typical unobtrusiveness which only the very wealthy can afford, Cindy found herself talking about herself and it was some time before she realised, rather ruefully, that she had been very discreetly quizzed.

The rest of the journey passed

comfortably, Cindy read some of the paperbacks she had brought with her and then found herself dozing as the effects of the almost constant supply of food took its toll.

It was dark when at last the plane began to descend. Straining for a view, Cindy saw the glitter where chains of lights stretched out beneath her. And then she felt the wheels touch down very gently, the rush of lights pass them as they raced along the runway. And at last, deceleration, the powerful grip of brakes before they rolled to a stop outside the reception building. She heaved a sigh of relief as she reached for the catch of her seat belt, then with the other passengers, began to search for her luggage.

It was all a mad bustle when they had disembarked. A confusion which was increased by the shock Cindy had felt when the door of the plane was thrown open letting in the night air. At first she had thought that it couldn't be true. Heat wasn't like this, not this suffocating, burning torment that tore the oxygen from your lungs before you could savour it.

By the time she had walked the few yards to the air-conditioned building the light cotton suit which had seemed so suitable when she left London was damp with sweat and sticking to her body. She felt the trickle run down her neck and between her breasts. Not for the first time she asked herself dejectedly just what she was doing here. There was no answer, so she decided that as soon as she possibly could do so, she must return to London.

Wearily she left the chatter of passengers waiting for their luggage. She went over to a pillar and leaned against it, gratefully pressing her body on the cool tiles, eyes closed.

She did not hear him come towards her so when he spoke, her eyes shot open. There was the trace of a smile on his lips as he looked at her and fascinated, she stared at his mouth.

'Miss Charles,' And to her ears it seemed that the pure English of his accent had been overlaid with something more exotic. 'Welcome to Arabia.'

A power that she could not defy was able to draw her eyes to his, to hold them for what seemed an age. Mingling with the green she fancied she saw flecks of gold but that probably was the effect of the lighting. Fascinated, she watched him, for the moment all her fatigue forgotten, then in an instinctively protective gesture, her hands moved to the stone of her pendant. She saw his eyes follow her movement, remain for a moment on the curve where her shirt clung damply before returning to her face. The smile had gone from his mouth but it lingered still in his voice as he repeated caressingly, almost sensuously. 'Welcome to Arabia.' Then experimentally, for the first time used her given name, 'Cindy.'

And the girl, leaning back against the pillar, recognised all the wild signals which she had been trying to ignore. This man meant danger. All her senses had been telling her so and she had been reckless to ignore the warnings. She should have stayed in London. For out here, what defence had she against him?

5

When she woke in her bed next morning, of course she was able to laugh at her fears. She lay in the cool perfection of her air-conditioned room and was able to smile at herself. Why she should have had that sudden image of danger, merely because he had used her name, she had no idea. In England, after all, she would have thought it strange if a man his age had persisted with the formality of Miss Charles.

And what for goodness' sake, did she expect him to do with her? Carry her off to some secret spot and make wild demanding love before sending her back on the next plane? She blushed, laughed and pulled the cool sheet up to her neck at the thought.

'Come in,' she called when someone tapped unexpectedly on the door.

A young woman, dressed in the

enveloping robes that were becoming so familiar came into the room and placed the small tray she was carrying down on the bedside table.

'Thank you.' Gratefully Cindy sat up and poured herself out a cup of the fragrant tea. She drank thirstily, looking around her as she did so.

Last night, after the drive from the airport and the meal that had been waiting for them, she had been too tired to do more than take briefest account of her surroundings. She had noticed with pleasure the charm of the courtyard where the retinue of cars had pulled up, her artist's eye approving the line of arches that enclosed the covered walkways forming the sides of the square. She had been aware of the cooling sound of water from the fountains in the centre and in each corner, of the white stone softly gleaming in the skilfully concealed lighting as they hurried from the car through the hot dark night.

Supper she had eaten without really

noticing what it had consisted of and then, excusing herself, she had said goodnight. She had addressed herself mainly to the Sheikha, scarcely daring to look too closely at the Sheikh who himself appeared to pay little attention to their guest.

Cindy threw back the light cover and got up. Although she had taken a few minutes for a quick shower last night, she couldn't resist the temptation of another before breakfast. And that meal which she had been told would be waiting for her whenever she felt like appearing in the dining-room was suddenly very tempting.

Twenty minutes later, fresh and pretty in a muslin dress the colour of ripe greengages, Cindy walked along the corridor and into the dining-room. She paused on the threshold, pleased to see that her recollection had not been at fault.

The room was cool and dim, protected from the glare of daylight by the arched walk which had made such a pleasing sight the previous evening. Like the rest of the house, it benefitted from the efficient air-conditioning system but unlike the bedroom at least, its style was entirely in keeping with the exterior of the house. It was lofty with a slightly domed ceiling and the walls were white, hung here and there with rugs in Turkey red and black. The floor was wood, golden in colour and planed to a smooth fineness. Against one wall was a cupboard in the same light wood but the table was what drew Cindy's gaze in ecstatic admiration. Green, almost like his eyes but not quite, she assured herself, determined to keep her thoughts from that particular path. Green marble round top with a border of jet about a foot from the edge.

She saw that two places were set, that a coffee pot stood on an electric hot plate. She went forward pulling out one of the honey wood chairs and sitting down. She had eaten the delicious concoction of fruit and was pouring herself a cup of coffee when the door opened quite suddenly and the Sheikh strode into the room. It was the first time that Cindy had seen him in any dress other than Arab and his appearance was so unsettling that she slopped some coffee into her saucer.

'Good morning, Miss Charles.' A sardonic eyebrow was raised at the spilled coffee. 'You slept well?' He pulled out the other chair and sat almost facing her.

'Very well, thank you.' She looked down at the piece of bread on her plate. Then, taking courage she raised her face to his. 'You have been riding?'

'Yes.' The cool green eyes appraised her, the white teeth gleamed briefly. 'You ride, Miss Charles?' There was something mocking about his formality.

'Yes, Sheikh Al Adham.' Deliberately she held his long cool gaze, reflecting that it was indecent to feel so disturbed this early in the morning. 'At least,' she amended, 'I used to. Since I came to London to live I haven't had much opportunity.'

'Then you must ride while you are here. When you have finished breakfast I shall take you to show you the stables. Then we can select a mount for your use while you are here with us.'

'Oh . . . I don't know. I have come here to work. Not to waste my time riding.' She shrugged apologetically. 'I don't know that Mr Gascoigne would approve.'

'Mr Gascoigne is not here to approve or disapprove so we shan't allow his opinions to influence us. What matters is whether or not you would like to do some riding.'

'Oh, I would.' Cindy felt herself relaxing. 'So long as we are speaking of horses. I don't know how I'd get on with camels.'

To her pleasure he put back his head and laughed. 'No, not camels. I shan't introduce you to those just yet. I think on the whole you'd do better on a horse.' He drained his cup and pushing back his chair stood up. 'If you've finished I'll take you to the stables.'

In that instant as she sat looking up at the tall figure dressed in pale riding breeches thrust into black boots and a white shirt open at the neck, Cindy remembered briefly that disturbing flash at the airport. But this morning, it seemed so ridiculously dramatic that she dismissed it and followed him meekly from the room.

They paused for a moment in the hall where the Sheikh went into a cloakroom and reappeared carrying a large straw hat, the kind with a scarf sewn inside, protecting not merely the top of the head but also the back of the neck.

'Here, wear that,' he looked at her blond hair in a way that made her begin to feel warm but turned away before the colour began to stain her skin. As she walked after him, she tied the ends of the scarf loosely beneath her chin.

When he opened the great heavy front door, the sudden ferocious heat was like a blow. Although after last night she expected it she flinched and the Sheikh, holding open the door for her noticed and put out a hand protectively.

'Steady. Come on this way.' With one hand under her arm, he led her swiftly into the shadows where the drifting spray from the fountains had cooled the atmosphere marginally. Then he stopped, turning her towards him, 'I can't say that you'll get used to it for you never do.' The green eyes bored into hers so that she felt faint, but still she was uncertain whether this was due to the heat or the touch of his hands on hers.

As if sensing some of her disturbance, his hands dropped but not before she had with an effort regained some of her self-control.

'That's a strange thing for you to say.' She smiled faintly. 'I should have thought you'd be quite used to it.'

He stared at her without answering for a moment. Then, slowly, 'Not I. But come,' he seemed to recover himself. 'It's foolish to linger about in the heat when we could be inside.' He grinned suddenly, 'I've heard visitors from Europe say that the heat in Riyadh can melt your brains. And that's in the cool season.' He went forward again but taking care, so she thought, not to leave her behind this time as he had yesterday at the airport.

The stables were reached eventually by going through an elegant wrought iron gate from the courtyard and along another covered passageway. Electric fans whirred high overhead in the clean group of buildings which comprised the garages and the stabling for more than a dozen horses.

Several grooms were busy about the place but one, apparently the senior, came forward when Cindy and the Sheikh stepped inside. The man looked suspiciously at the girl through jet black eyes set in a face of wrinkled brown leather then turned as his employer spoke rapidly, obviously explaining that they were looking for a suitable mount for the visitor.

Again the man turned his unsmiling

gaze on the girl, seemed rapidly to take note of her height and build before pointing towards the far end of the stable. The Sheikh, obviously in agreement, nodded, then led Cindy further on.

'Yes, Abdul is right of course.' He stopped at the last stall. 'This would be the best choice for you, I think.'

Cindy looked at the beautiful mare, saw the creamy head turn, felt an immediate sympathy between herself and the horse. Nevertheless, the animal was of such obvious quality and breeding that she felt she daren't accept the offer.

'Oh, isn't she gorgeous!' She stepped forward to stroke the fine pale coat, allowed the soft mouth to nuzzle against her hand. 'But,' she raised her head to look at the man across the animal's back. 'I couldn't possibly ride her.' She shrugged. 'I'm afraid she's out of my class.' As she saw the eyebrows opposite raised she smiled, 'I'm sorry, my riding was confined to the pony club hacks. That and an old mare which I kept for a few years before I went to college. I just wouldn't feel safe riding such a valuable animal.'

'You need not worry about that. She is quite a docile creature.'

'Oh, I didn't mean that. I wouldn't be worrying about myself. It's the horse I would be worrying about.'

'Yes, I understood exactly what you meant. And what I meant was that neither of you would come to any harm. I trust you both. Implicitly.' He added after a pause.

'Oh . . . Thank you.' The look in his eyes was confusing and she looked away from him to where her hand was stroking the silky back.

'Then that is agreed. And of course you will not ride during the heat of the day. Very early morning and in the evenings are the best times. I usually ride about six. So . . . ' there seemed to be a challenge in his manner, ' . . . If you care to join me then, Miss Charles?'

'Thank you.' Still she seemed to be concentrating her attention on the horse with more intensity than it required.

'Come then.' Abruptly he forced her to look at him. 'We can return to the house this way . . . ' He indicated another door, before turning to speak a few words to Abdul who was still hovering nearby. The groom nodded once or twice, then a grin, somewhat reluctant touched his lips as his glance slid round to Cindy.

'That's all right then.' The Sheikh nodded a dismissal as he led the way to the door at the end of the row of stalls. 'I've told him that you're to have the use of Hasa while you are here.' He paused while she walked through the door he held open for her. 'Perhaps you would like to see the hounds while we are here.' As he spoke there came the sound of excited barking from an adjoining building and when they went in, the man was at once surrounded by yelping dogs. For a moment he fondled the nearest, until a few firm words brought them under control and they edged back, sitting in a rough semi-circle in front of them.

'Salukis,' the Sheikh explained. 'You won't see many dogs here. Muslims think they are unclean. Only the saluki is allowed for hunting.

'Oh, I see.' Cindy put out a tentative hand to touch the nearest on the muzzle. 'They sounded very fierce.'

'Well, they're pack animals and here they are working dogs, not domestic pets. That's the best kind of life for animals.' He went to the door and opened it, clearly impatient to be attending his own affairs instead of acting as guide to an employee. Meekly Cindy followed although she was irritated by his sudden change of mood.

But as they walked across towards the house, she found that she had been mistaken in her assumptions.

'I've just realised, Miss Charles, that I'm late for an appointment in Riyadh. Not,' his teeth behind the tiny beard gleamed momentarily, 'not that that will surprise anyone here. Manana might have been invented by the Saudis. Only here they say 'Bukra Insha'llah', Tomorrow God willing. It's very convenient to have God to blame!'

Thankfully, Cindy walked through the door he held open into the cool interior of the house. She was slightly amused by the way he always spoke about things here as if he himself were divorced from them. The smile she turned on him was unconsciously dazzling but she saw his eyes move to her hair as she took off the hat, moving her head slightly to loosen the constrictions caused by the scarf. All at once, in the dim intimacy of the corridor, she felt breathless. Although aware of her dress clinging damply to her, she tried to be casual.

'Thank you, Sheikh Al Adham for showing me the stables.'

'And tomorrow?' The green eyes moved from her hair to her face. 'You will ride with me?'

'If . . . If you do not mind.' There was nothing casual about the way her pulses were hammering.

'I am inviting you so . . . clearly I do not mind.' Somewhere far away, a woman laughed, the sound drifting along the corridor towards them. He turned away with a curious little sigh. 'Now, I expect that my mother will be awake. I think she has plans to take you to visit Nevine today. But I think that I must warn you, Miss Charles, that,' they began to stroll along the corridor, 'so far you have seen only Westernised Arabs. They are the exceptions.'

It was difficult to know what he meant, impossible to comment.

'Of course.' The answer meant whatever he wanted it to mean.

They had come to the main hall and clearly he was impatient to go. 'I shall ring for a maid and she will take you to my mother's apartments.' He paused with one finger on a bell concealed in the carved panelling.

'Thank you, Sheikh.'

112

'Sheikh . . . means old man. Did you know that, Miss Charles?'

From his tone she was unable to decide whether or not he was complaining. She shook her head without replying.

'Do you consider it suitable for me?'

She tried to disguise the smile, but failed. 'No.' This time her head shook with more firmness.

'Then please do not use the title to me, Miss Charles. Really, I do not deserve it.' Although his manner was completely serious she knew that he was teasing.

'I shall try not to. But . . . ' the thought had just occurred to her, 'what should I call you then?'

'You,' and there was the faintest emphasis on that word, 'may call me Adham. It is, after all, my name.' He stepped away from the wall, so that they stood close together again. 'But in return then I expect to be allowed to call you something more friendly than Miss Charles.'

There wasn't a sound as she looked up at him but she was remembering last night at the airport when he had used her first name, thinking of the pleasure it had brought her.

'Cindy.' He spoke it again. But this time as if he did not much like it. 'This is your only name?'

She nodded. 'Yes. Lucinda Charles.'

'Lucinda, of course. That suits you much better. Then if I may, I shall call you Lucinda.' And before she could say another word, he had turned and opened the door letting in the burning air of the desert.

★　★　★

Cindy stood for a moment looking at the closed door, then she drew in a shuddering breath. She was letting this man get under her skin and if she didn't get a grip on herself she would find that it would be impossible to get on with the work she had come to do. With a determination wholly assumed, she took a step across and pressed the concealed bell firmly. There was no sense in wasting time. The sooner she found out what was expected of her, the sooner she would be able to fly back to London. And away from . . . away from disturbing influences.

*　*　*

Cindy was bewildered by the city which they drove through. She sat in the back beside the Sheikha listening as the soft voice went on describing the area through which they were passing. But to the girl, Riyadh resembled nothing so much as a vast building site. Wherever the eye turned, huge cranes defaced the skyline, here and there were buildings which had been begun and then abandoned. As if to assure herself that what she was seeing was really there, Cindy pushed her dark glasses to the top of her head and sat forward staring through the tinted glass of the limousine.

'I see that you are disappointed.' There was a sigh in the Sheikha's voice as she correctly interpreted the visitor's reaction. 'Ah well, I'm afraid that will be the general response until this present mad building boom bursts.'

'I had not realised . . . We hear a lot about it at home but somehow . . . ' Her voice trailed away.

'If only you could have seen it twenty years ago. But there, we mustn't pretend that things haven't improved in other ways. Life for the majority is so much better on the whole. Only . . . ' the Sheika smiled, 'we older ones regret the passing of the things that we associate with our youth. I just consider we are lucky that the rebuilding has not affected us unduly. On the outskirts of the town where we are, things are comparatively unchanged.'

'Yes, it is very peaceful out there. I didn't hear a thing when I went to bed last night.'

'Of course you were exhausted. I could see that.' The dark eyes looked at the girl appraisingly. 'But it's clear that the sleep has restored you completely. Now,' she sat forward on her seat as the car turned in through a high arched gateway and into a courtyard, 'we have arrived. You have your sketch books, Cindy? Then we shall go in and you can meet Nevine.'

The step from the air-conditioned car to the cool dim hall left Cindy gasping and wondering distractedly how she was going to manage with the restricted wardrobe she had brought with her. She felt a moment's envy of the Sheikha with her loose and presumably cool robes and as if in response to her thoughts, her companion turned to her sympathetically.

'You must find the heat a great trial, Cindy. And there don't seem to be any European clothes that can cope with it. Your cotton dresses are very pretty but . . . ' she smiled, 'I don't suppose you'd care to go 'native' while you're here?'

'I was just thinking how much more

117

suitable your clothes are.' Cindy laughed ruefully. 'But I think you have to be born to them. I'm sure I shouldn't be able to manage them. But I was wondering what I was going to do. Already I'm on to my second dress of the day.'

'There's no need to worry about that. The one you left off will be washed and ironed by now. There are plenty of servants so you need not feel guilty. In fact they like doing things for visitors. Ah,' she turned when a soft-footed servant came across the hall towards them, 'here is Yusup.' As the Sheikha spoke to the man, Cindy saw that instinctively she held a fold of her robes across her face. No matter how Westernised, how sophisticated one was, apparently all those early years of conditioning had an effect that was impossible to eradicate.

'That is all right. Yusup is going to fetch one of the maids . . . '

Yusup clapped his hands and at once, from the shadows under one of the arched alcoves, a figure shrouded in black came towards them. Her outline was entirely shapeless and almost all that could be seen of her face was the pair of coal black eyes. Cindy feeling awkward and conspicuous in the midst of all this modesty followed with the Sheikha as the woman led the way along a corridor and in through a door which she held open for them.

They were in a large, low-ceilinged room, all white except for the large divan in shades of deep red, two matching chairs and a long table with a tiled top. At the far side of the room, towards the windows, was a fretwork screen and as she stood just inside the door, Cindy saw a figure rise from a seated position behind the screen and then emerge into the room.

When she saw the young woman, for strangely she did not doubt that this was Nevine, Cindy heard a rushing sound in her ears and for a moment thought that she would faint. But her swimming senses cleared as she saw the

Sheikha go forward to greet her niece. Then, with an arm round the figure dressed in dark green, she pulled her gently forward.

'Nevine, this is Cindy who has come out from England specially to design some jewellery for your wedding. Cindy, this is my niece.'

It was almost impossible to see what was going on behind that hideous mask. All Cindy could see was the curve of the chin, the gleam of particularly lustrous dark eyes through the slits.

Nervously she swallowed. 'How do you do?' It was, she thought, a singularly idiotic thing to say but to her surprise there was a gurgle of laughter from behind the mask and the voice that spoke, while not as fluent in English as the Sheikha was certainly no stranger to the language.

'How shocked you look! Do you mean to say that no one warned you that you would meet a barqad woman?'

And as Cindy looked at the black

helmet which covered the hair and almost the entire face of the girl, she knew that here, she had met something which she could never understand.

6

Back in the room which had been arranged for her sketching, Cindy tried to keep her mind firmly fixed on what she was trying to do. Only, unfortunately, all she could see in her mind was the thing she wished she could wipe completely from her mind.

For she felt that the rest of her life would be haunted by the sight of that young girl, defaced, yes, she decided that was not too strong a word, defaced by that awful mask. And although the girl herself was apparently unaware of the indignity, the humiliation of the situation, Cindy was convinced that that was simply because she did not understand her position.

She shivered slightly as she reached for her drawing pen. How was it possible for her to design light-hearted jewellery for a girl in that situation?

Surely if she thought of the bride at all, she was bound to find her imagination running in the direction of binding chains and severe padlocks. Impatient with herself, she tossed down the pen and leaned her head in her hands. With an effort she forced her mind away from her meeting with Nevine. The only way she was going to be able to fulfil her contract was to think of some other person about to be married, someone like Marjorie ... With a sigh of relief she reached again for the pen.

★ ★ ★

By the end of the week, Cindy felt that she was on the threshold of completing some of her best work. Once she had made a start, ideas seemed to flow from the end of her pen with ease. Her first batch of sketches were inspired by thoughts of Marjorie but they did not satisfy her for long and soon were discarded in favour of an entirely different series.

She was so totally absorbed in what she was doing that she worked straight through the day without a break and nothing that the Sheikha could say or do would dissuade her.

'You see, Sheikha,' Cindy murmured abstractedly when the other protested, 'I've always found it easy to sketch when the ideas are there.' She tapped her forehead with a slightly ink-stained finger. 'If you postpone it till later, sometimes you can find that they have gone, leaving a total blank.' She tapped her teeth with the pen.

'Well,' the Sheikha's tolerant expression was lost on the girl, 'I shall see that you have plenty of fruit and coffee. If you can eat some of the chicken that the maid has brought,' she gestured with one of her delicate hands towards the tray that had been left on a small table, 'but I shall leave you. Oh, by the way,' She turned as she reached the door, 'I did tell you that my son will be with us tonight for dinner?'

Cindy's hand paused in the middle of

making a stroke. Then slowly she swung round to face the Sheikha. 'I'm sorry, what did you say?' But the colour was flooding her cheeks.

'Merely that Adham will be with us tonight. So it will perhaps be less dull for you than for the last few evenings.' The door closed behind her.

Alone in the room, Cindy sat for a moment trying to control the impatient beating of her heart. So, he would be coming back. Back to disturb her again, to distract her from what she was trying to do. She had been grateful, she insisted to herself, that an unexpected summons had made him dash off hurriedly to Kuwait a few days ago. For only then had she been able to get down to doing some work.

But now, presumably he would be constantly in and out of the house; she would be bumping into him, and more disturbingly, expecting to bump into him, each time she turned a corner in one of the corridors. And presumably, her mind reared nervously at the thought, she would be expected to join him in the mornings to ride. It had been so much less distracting these last few days to rise at dawn and to take Hasa, already saddled for her, from the stable and ride out and round the perimeter of the grounds on her own.

That first morning, when she had joined him just as a faint blush stained the eastern horizon had not made for an easy relaxing day. The combination of the desert and the man had been just too heady for comfort. Not that he had been aware of it. And she was fairly certain that she hadn't betrayed herself. But it hadn't been easy and she was uncertain of her reactions in the future.

He had been waiting for her in the stables, had nodded approvingly, his eyes moving over her slim figure dressed in pink jeans and a long-sleeved cream shirt. Her hair had been enveloped in the concealing hat and her sunglasses were in her hand.

'I see you're learning.' With a smile he turned from her, spoke a few words to the stable boy who led the horses out into the courtyard.

He held Hasa's head while she mounted, then a moment later he was astride his dark coloured stallion while Cindy followed him out into the desert. He showed her first round the boundary of the property, marked, rather roughly Cindy thought, by a few trees and the odd bush. Away to the left she could just discern the scatter of buildings that marked the nearest outskirts of Riyadh, to the right, the desert, the edge of nothingness.

At the stunted palm tree farthest from the house, he stopped, turning his mount so that he could look at her, the green eyes narrowed slightly. He was etched against the pink dawn as he leaned forward to clasp the bridle of her horse. 'You want to see the desert?' It was more a statement than a question but she answered, almost mesmerised.

'Yes.' From the pocket of her blouse she pulled her sun-glasses and put them on, hoping rather despairingly that they would offer some protection.

'Then, come with me, Lucinda.' He paused while his eyes continued to hold hers dominantly. 'And I shall show it to you.' Quite abruptly he turned, his hand dropping the rein. Without stirring she watched him move ahead, saw the tall figure dressed in riding breeches and white shirt, the dark hair lifting slightly with the motion of the horse. They might she thought, have been in England, so English did he seem.

Then with a twitch of her reins she followed, concentrating as she followed him along an unmarked path which rambled across the desert. And the desert . . . What could she think of that? It was so different from what she had imagined. So disappointing? She asked herself that as she rode swiftly in pursuit of the Sheikh. Certainly different, she qualified. She hadn't really expected vast expanses of soft sand such as you find on beaches in Cornwall. On the other hand neither had she thought it would be quite so dingy, quite so rock-strewn and rough.

'Disappointed?' He had stopped to wait for her and not noticing she had almost bumped into him. He smiled at her discomforture, amusement gleaming in his eyes and showing in the sudden flash of white teeth in the darkness of the beard.

'Of course not.' Politeness forced the words from her lips.

'Curious.' He held his head to one side disbelievingly. 'Most people are. But here . . . ' he pointed one finger ahead, 'here is a main camel run.' Again he smiled and this time she could see that he was laughing at himself. Unable to resist, she allowed her gaze to linger over his mouth. 'And here,' he seemed not to have noticed, 'we can let ourselves really go.'

With that he dug his knees into his horse's side, the animal snorted, reared slightly shaking his head and then was streaking down the flat hard dirt road. Cindy followed more sedately, still not entirely certain that Hasa was as calm and equable as everyone seemed to think. But at the end of about a mile, when she saw the Sheikh waiting for her, she pulled up feeling exhilarated and madly adventurous.

'This way now.' Again he took her bridle and led her up a small incline, behind which she could just make out the tops of a few palm trees. When they reached the top of the rise, they stopped and Cindy drew in her breath in a sudden gasp. For there in front of them was the perpetual image of the desert.

A small round water hole fringed by date palms, now outlined in black against the fiery ball of the rising sun. Slowly she urged the horse forward and this time the Sheikh allowed her to go ahead. When she reached the edge of the pool, she slipped from the saddle, then felt the reins taken from her.

'Go and drink.' It was a command. 'The water is sweet.'

Without waiting to be told how, she lay down flat, cupping the clear water in her hands, drinking and allowing the cool liquid to spill down her chin and run cool inside her blouse. When she had satisfied her thirst, she turned on her back to find him standing looking down, a curious expression on his face which at once brought her heart hammering into her throat.

'I — I've always wanted to do that.' Her laugh was uncertain. 'To drink from an oasis, just once in my lifetime.'

'And . . . ' To her ears there seemed a wealth of meaning in his words, 'and did it come up to your expectations?'

The words which came were not the ones she longed to speak. She said, pausing as if to savour the taste of the water. 'Yes. There's a tang of — of salt I think.'

She longed to tell him that the desert was fulfilling all her wildest dreams, so long as she was seeing it with him.

'Then,' frowning he looked towards the horses, 'if you will hold them while I drink . . . '

'Of course.' Hastily she jumped up,

131

conscious that she had disappointed, taking the reins, trying to ignore the fire that his touch aroused in her.

When he had finished drinking he stood up, wiping his mouth and indicating that she should release the impatient horses. This she did with some relief for the stallion was no easy animal to control. Together they watched their greedy drinking before with mutual agreement they turned away.

'That of course is bad practice . . . ' With a glance at her look of enquiry he went on, 'All true Bedu would have allowed their animals to drink first. But now, his shrug was expressive, 'we are too squeamish to drink after our horses.' He leaned against one of the trees and she watched as he searched in a pocket for a cheroot, saw the flick of flame as his lighter fired. He sighed, expelling the smoke from his lungs then following with his eyes its slow dispersal in the still air.

'And you,' Cindy made an effort to

regain his attention, 'do not consider yourself one? A true Bedu?' She tried not to feel foolish as she spoke the unfamiliar word.

Instantly the green eyes were turned towards her, ravishing in their painful intensity. In that moment they seemed to spark such fire that mentally she recoiled but then he gave a short, bitter little laugh.

'Come, Lucinda.' The cruel note in his voice mocked them both, she thought. 'I have shown you an oasis at sunrise. Not quite the Taj Mahal by moonlight perhaps, but then we can't have everything can we?'

There was such an ache in her chest that she could only shake her head. Then quite suddenly he smiled again, his normal friendly smile and the ache disappeared as swiftly as it had come. He helped her to mount then sprang confidently into the saddle, turning his prancing horse round and quietening him with a sharp command.

'Come, Cindy . . . ' He stopped and

made a rueful grimace. 'There, it looks as if I've begun to think of you as Cindy after all. Perhaps we should try to accept things as they are and not try to change them.' He grinned at her. 'I'm full of wise sayings this morning. It must be the effect of the desert in the dawn. With a pretty girl.'

And following him along the track, Cindy found that her heart was singing wildly.

★   ★   ★

But the desert, although it sometimes gave the impression of drab colourlessness, had a bewitching variety all of its own. Cindy found this on the subsequent days when she roamed about in the early mornings watching the effect of the sun as it rose sluggishly over the horizon.

Yes, that was when she first began to be aware of the strange compelling magic of the desert, as she sat watching the sun rise, casting deep shadows, its rays searching out the crannies in the dun coloured sand. Searching them out then changing them to tiny jewelled boxes brimming over with all the subtlest kinds of gem. More than once, Cindy dismounted, convinced that she had discovered a tiny cache of quartz or beryl. But each time the colours faded as she reached out, disappearing, reverting to the familiar drabness.

But the artist's eye was captivated by the almost magical effects, entranced by the changes wrought by the strengthening slanted rays. So, often she was content merely to sit, quite still, her back supported against a tree, Hasa lightly tethered in some shade, while she watched, fascinated by the changing shifting pattern of colours, more varied and exciting than any she could have imagined. And all brought about by the refraction of light on this most unpromising material, this dull, nothing-coloured sand.

And so in those quiet hours, the desert began to weave its spell about her, began to spin strands that would always bind her. But more important to her at that moment, the desert fired her imagination, the experience invaded her work, making her pen fly over the paper with a jumble of ideas. Ideas which would later require controlling, modifying. Until at last, delicately sketched they could be presented as the enchanting designs which would be called the Nevine Collection.

★　★　★

But that was still some way in the future. On the day when the Sheikha had told Cindy that her son would be with them that evening, she herself had to leave unexpectedly after the light mid-day meal which Cindy for once ate in the dining-room with her hostess.

'I am so sorry to have to leave you, Cindy,' said the Sheikha when she had explained the matter to the girl. 'To be truthful I would much rather not rush off to Istanbul right now. If it were not that my sister sounded so 'distraite' on the telephone.' She wrinkled her nose charmingly. 'It is such a worry to us. You will perhaps understand better now that you have been here for some time. Divorce in itself is such a disgrace here. For a woman! Then to marry someone who is half-Jewish.' She gave a little shudder. 'And although my sister is most happily married and her husband is charming . . . ' The sigh was more expressive than any prolonged explanation would have been. 'Well, she longs for home and that is exactly what she cannot have. So, I try to be indulgent and when things get too much for her, I go running. But I have told her that I shall stop only two nights. I feel so sorry that I have to go, my dear. But I know that Adham will be home and he will look after you.'

Cindy tried to conceal the tumult of feeling that rose inside her as she heard the Sheikha's words. She was silent for a time, appearing to be absorbed in the apple that she was peeling before looking up at her hostess with a smile. 'Of course I understand that you must go, Sheikha. If your sister is ill. In fact,' Again she looked down at her plate, 'I really feel I ought to be thinking of going home, too. I have made such a lot of sketches and I was hoping that perhaps tomorrow you could come to some decision . . .'

'Are you so anxious to leave us, my dear?' The woman's dark eyes were intent on the girl. 'I had hoped that perhaps you would think of your stay here as something of a holiday. But you have been so industrious . . .'

There was a little laugh from Cindy. 'Oh, it's as I told you the other day, when the inspiration is there you daren't ignore it. But I do feel that it's time I went back to London. When I wrote to Mr Gascoigne the other day I told him that I would soon be finished.'

'Oh, then when I come back we must decide. But I shall leave a message for my son that he must see you are properly entertained for the last few days. He has so many westernised friends in the city . . . It would be a pity if you did not meet them. And perhaps he would take you in to see Nevine again. I know that she enjoyed meeting you and would like to see you before you go.'

So when she was left alone in the house except for the servants, Cindy had the prospect of two very different meetings ahead of her. One that filled her with a trembling excited expectation, not unmixed with dread, and the other which must fall very firmly into the category of duty. She had little inclination to see again the pathetic spectacle of a girl in barqa.

All that afternoon, Cindy spent at her drawing board, putting tiny last minute details on the sketches she had prepared. As she worked she sang lightly to herself, quite unaware that was she doing so but all the time listening for the stir in the corridors that would indicate that the master had returned.

But when teatime came and the girl came bringing the usual tray with a pot of fragrant scented tea, slices of lemon and ice water, Cindy threw her pen down with a sigh. She had done enough work to satisfy the most demanding taskmaster and she knew that nothing she could do would improve what she had done.

Slowly she drank the tea, savouring its refreshing tang, then when she had finished drinking, she stretched in an excess of relief and anticipation. Trying to still her rising excitement, she decided it was unlikely that she would see Adham before dinner. After his long spell of travelling and business dealings it was probable his first inclination would be to rest. And that, she thought, was an idea she might very well copy.

It was several hours later when Cindy woke up in the large luxurious bed-room. For a moment she lay without moving on the low divan type bed, only her eyes travelling over the room, struck for the umpteenth time by the absolute luxury of her surroundings.

'But you'd better not get too used to it, Cindy,' she admonished. 'A few days more and you'll be back to normal.' She struggled to a sitting position, swinging her feet on to the thick carpet. 'But it's amazing just how quickly you can adapt to it.' She padded across the large room and threw open the bathroom door. 'It'll be back to the cupboard soon.' She surveyed herself in the mirrored walls and then turned away to the shower.

Ten minutes later, she was back in the bedroom, sitting in front of the wide dressing table, drying her hair with the drier which had been thoughtfully provided. She remembered her surprise when she had first been shown into the room. Although she had had no preconceived ideas she had not expected this typically glossy magazine type of bedroom. But on the first day the Sheikha had told her that they had hired one of London's most influential young designers to come and completely redo their bedrooms.

It must be a habit of theirs, thought Cindy, thinking of her own situation.

But as far as the interior design went it had been extremely successful. The daring colour scheme in her room, dark green, almost black walls with dazzling white paint, might have been a total disaster but in fact it was extremely restful after the glare from the sun. The furniture was mainly high quality built-in units, white and gold and for contrast, several silk covered armchairs, one peacock blue and two pink.

By the time she was ready, it was almost eight o'clock and Cindy decided that there was no need to wait in her room any longer. Although her ear had been attuned to any sounds of arrival, she had heard none and had no idea whether or not the Sheikh had come back.

But it was unlikely that she would have heard in any case for she knew that his bedroom was on the opposite side of the house and it was probably that he would have gone straight there.

Before she turned towards the door, she stood in front of the mirror, trying to see herself as she thought he might. Her hair gleamed softly, falling in loose waves to her shoulders. With the touch of brown eyeshadow she had used, her eyes seemed larger and darker than normal and she hoped that he would not connect their limpid emotional look with himself. The dress she had chosen was one she had not worn before. Even now she was uncertain that it was suitable. Was it perhaps too exotic for a quiet evening 'at home' as it were? Would he think that she had worn it in a blatant attempt to engage his attention?

With a restless little shrug, she thrust the idea away from her and turned to the door. A faint flush lingered on her cheeks, an excited pulse throbbed in her veins as she opened the bedroom door and walked out into the corridor.

The house was still but when she reached the hall, she could hear a subdued chatter from the direction of the kitchen and Mohammed, the tall, bearded servant who normally guarded the door padded silently across, favouring her as he always did with a disapproving stare. For a while Cindy sat in the sitting-room, leafing through some of the magazines that seemed to be available in Arabia just as soon as they were in London or New York. But after a time she decided to go back to her room to fetch the paperback book she had thought of reading the previous night.

Just as she was returning, she had reached the hall again, when she heard the sound of car doors slamming, felt the hot blast of air as the front door was opened and she hesitated in the shadows, all at once overcome with shyness at the thought of meeting him again. The noise of her heart was loud in her ears but she tried to forget that and clasping the book firmly she prepared to step forward.

Then, she suddenly realised that the hall was filled with robed figures, the air was heavy with the aromatic smoke from many cigarettes and noisy with the sounds of argument and laughter. It was a moment before the significance of this dawned on her but the sight of Adham, tall and immaculate in white thobe leading his guests along the opposite corridor confirmed her fears.

In a moment she was back in her room, leaning against the door, her breast heaving. Slowly she walked across the floor and stood staring at herself again. What price now, she wondered, the beautiful dress? She smoothed a hand down over the sea-green silk. Then with a little frown of self-disgust she turned away. You fool, Cindy, she thought. Why should he be hurrying home to see you? You hardly know each other. And certainly you ought to know by this time, that in Arabia the men are the people who count. Women are very much second class citizens. Useful enough in their way. But she needn't imagine that Adham would forego a night with his friends in order to enjoy her company. Oh well. She certainly wasn't going to sit down and weep about it. Firmly she walked over to the bell set behind one of the curtains and pressed. When the girl came she would tell her to bring some food to the bedroom. And after that . . . Well, she would make up her mind after she had eaten. Meantime . . . She undid the long zip of her dress, it was time to get out of this idiotic get-up.

7

An hour later, Cindy, dressed in jeans and a long-sleeved silk shirt walked swiftly across in the direction of the stables. She couldn't imagine why she hadn't thought of it before. Riding across the desert under the stars was a perfect way to pass an evening. Tonight seemed hotter than ever but once she and the horse were in motion it would be less like a Turkish bath. And it was certainly wonderfully romantic with the stars strung across a dark blue velvet sky and the moon hanging full and heavy just above the horizon. It was the kind of night in England when one would fill one's lungs with great satisfying gulps of fresh air. But here . . . In relief, Cindy hurried into the buildings.

She didn't know the young man, a stable boy she presumed, whom she disturbed as she pushed open the heavy wooden door. He was lying on a sort of truckle bed, merely some thongs of webbing interlaced and strung across a wooden frame. He got up, turning down the volume of his transistor as he did so. He stood awkwardly, clutching his striped thobe about him. Cindy smiled and walked across to where Hasa was standing quietly. She rubbed her nose, gave her an apple which had come from her supper tray and then turned to the boy, telling him that she wanted the horse to be saddled.

But the boy appeared to be too intrigued by her face to hear or understand what she was saying for he made no move. In an effort to demonstrate more clearly, Cindy lifted down the saddle from the frame where it was kept and began to put it on the horse herself. At this the youth began to talk volubly and Cindy could see that he was trying to dissuade her from her decision. In fact he would have taken the saddle back if she hadn't held on to it insistently. The boy kept pointing towards the door and she imagined that he was saying that it was too late for riding. But she merely laughed, continued with her efforts to push the stiff leather straps through the buckles until in the end with an expressive shrug he gave in and began to help.

But again, when he opened the door for her, he pointed to the sky and made some obviously dissuading remark. Cindy decided to humour him. 'Yes, I know it's late. But I shan't go far. I shall be back before you even realise that I've gone.' She smiled, dug her heels lightly into Hasa's sides and trotted off.

It had been a great idea and just what she needed to restore her to her senses. The little horse moved with sure-footed smoothness over the ground and by and by, the girl felt some of her pain and yes, she might as well call it what it was, resentment slip away from her. There was nothing like physical exercise for restoring a sense of balance.

She rode all round the perimeter,

then pulling on the reins, she headed back again. In spite of her inclination to ride hard and fast out into the desert, the boy's admonition had had some effect. It was growing late and she didn't know the country. She made another circuit of the grounds, then she sat for a time looking forward to where the moon, white and mysterious, looked down on an empty world.

It was then she remembered the oasis. She knew exactly where it was, less than two miles away and with the moon reflected in the dark still waters it would be magical. And there was no one out there. The Sheikh had told her so. 'It's called The Empty Quarter. A huge barren void between here and Muscat. They say you could travel for weeks in any one direction without meeting a living soul.'

So that, thought Cindy making up her mind in an instant, means that it is safe. She turned the horse's head round to face into the tiny breeze that had unexpectedly blown up and set off in the direction of the flat dirt road.

The moon made it as clear as day and she had no difficulty in finding the route. It was a little less pleasant than she had imagined, riding out in the moonlight for the wind seemed to be lifting the sand, tossing it like small barbs against her skin. She unwound the scarf part of her hat and readjusted it so that her face was almost completely enclosed. Hasa too appeared to be finding it less than pleasant for she was making whinnying little sounds of protest and tossed her head from time to time as if trying to clear the grit from her eyes.

But they were nearly there now, Cindy could see the tops of the palms above the rise and with a sigh of relief she realised that the hill was giving them some protection from the searching little breeze. Hasa hurried down the path to the water and before the girl could stop her she began to drink greedily from the hole.

'That's all right.' Cindy laughed and

slid down with relief. She patted the animal's silky flank, 'You must be thirsty after all that dust.' As if to underline that, Hasa at once began to make coughing noises in between the loud slurps of water so that Cindy decided that perhaps after all, she would wait until she reached home before quenching her own thirst. About her, she heard the wind give a long moaning sob and in that instant the moon was suddenly obscured like a light that had been abruptly switched off.

'Hasa!' There was a note of panic in her voice as she pulled on the rein which she was still holding, drawing the horse close to her. The mare showed her impatience by the prancing little movements, by the whinnying and the tossing of her head. The girl, by now no less anxious than the horse, forced herself to speak gently while she searched for the stirrup and then swung herself into the saddle. At once, with a frightened snort, Hasa was trotting up the small incline that would take them at once back on to the hard road.

'Good girl.' In relief Cindy leaned forward to pat encouragingly, and at that very moment, as they crested the hill, they were seized, horse and rider by a whirling maelstrom of sand that left them without sight or breath. Cindy had heard of sand storms but at that moment she was too bemused by the sudden shock to understand what was happening. Only some instinct of self-preservation made her put her head down and wind her arms round the animal's neck.

Soothingly she continued to murmur, hoping that her own panic would not be recognised. And then, just as she sensed that the horse was calming, there was a jolt as Hasa stumbled, catapulting her rider on to the story ground.

The sound of retreating hoofs was soon swallowed in the hissing swooping scream of the wind. Stunned, the girl lay for a moment, sick with misery at the realisation that she had lost the

Sheikh's valuable horse.

But even that consideration didn't trouble her long for her own situation was becoming increasingly uncomfortable and dangerous. Tentatively at last she moved, relieved to find herself unhurt and slowly began to struggle to her feet. The wind was a screaming tormenting devil now, its breath a furnace, castigating the skin, threatening the eyes.

There was no escape from its terrible pressure for whichever way she turned, it clawed ferociously. Desperately trying to protect herself from its savagery, the girl began to pull the hat down over her face, to bring the scarf forward a little. As she struggled to adjust the knot, with an almost demonic scream of rage, the wind tore it from her grasp and in an instant, it was gone. Hair lashed about her face in a frenzy.

With a hopeless little sob, Cindy sank down on to her knees. She had no idea where she was, which way she ought to turn. If she attempted to move, it was even possible that she might fall into the pool. Face down she lay on the ground, her arms wound protectively about her streaming hair.

What had seemed like a romantic defiant gesture when she left home she now saw for what it was, the action of a spoiled foolish child. She shuddered when she thought what form the Sheikh's anger might take. And an even more unpleasant thought . . . probably no one had the slightest idea where she was. It was unlikely that the stable boy would trouble to go up to the house to let them know that she had ridden off against all advice. No doubt when, or if — she corrected her jumbled thoughts — if Hasa returned to the stable the boy would still hesitate about his next move. Probably he would allow some time to elapse before taking any action. And by that time . . . Her mind veered from such speculation.

★　★　★

For a long time Cindy lay where she was on the hard sand. For part of the time she drifted into a restless sleep but even there she found no escape from her bitter self-reproach. She saw in her dreams Adham going to the door of her bedroom and when there was no response to his knocking, he pushed it open. Inside, as he noticed the discarded dress, the undisturbed bed, his face changed to one of concern, despair even. But at that point in the repeated dream, Cindy always wakened to the realisation that her situation was unchanged and she had no reason to imagine that Adham would think to go to her room. Even if he made inquiries, which she had no right to think he would, the maid would be certain to tell him that she had taken a meal to Cindy's room. She would be assumed to have gone to sleep.

Painfully, Cindy raised her head from the stony ground. The wind seemed scarcely to have abated and as soon as her face was exposed, the sand like tiny spears struck her skin. Nevertheless, she continued to hold her head in an attentive listening position. For in her fevered imaginings she thought that she had heard someone call. She felt her eyes become encrusted with salty grains as the wind tore her eyelids open.

There it was again. Her heart began to hammer in an excess of revived hope. Summoning all her strength, she struggled to her knees and faced in the direction from which she thought the sound had come. It almost burst her lungs to fight the wind, to shout as loudly as she could. Tears came to her eyes when she realised that only a croak issued from her cracked lips, her parched throat.

Then another call, not her own, came faintly towards her through the dust and this time she recognised it as her own name. The sound came whipping towards her and seemed marginally nearer. At the same time, a faint light began to penetrate the Stygian gloom and then to increase.

A moment later, he was beside her and although she couldn't distinguish either shape or features, she had no doubt who he was. With a silent prayer of thankfulness, she took his hand, leaning slightly towards him. But his manner showed none of the tender relief that she could have been hoping for.

His hands were rough and impersonal as he pulled her towards him and lifted her on to the back of the horse he was leading. She heard the nervous animal snort restlessly, paw the ground in protest before Adham with a word of firm command sprang into the saddle behind Cindy. His arms were firm round her waist and with a tiny sigh of relief, she relaxed against him, grateful for the enveloping protection of the long cloak which he drew about them both. All at once she was safe. The storm ceased to matter now that she was so close to him.

Vaguely she heard him coax the horse forward, felt the reluctant stumbling steps as the huge animal moved forward into the darkness. About them the wind still screamed and howled with undiminished fury and clearly the stallion was totally unnerved by this example of nature at its most violent. A step at a time they moved forward, the man coaxing, gentle, the horse reluctant, as if dreading what each move might encounter.

She had no idea how long they tried to find protection from the storm, she was aware only of relief that someone was here who would look after her. For the moment it was all that mattered. That and knowing that it was Adham's heart beating strongly against her cheek.

It was a deep weary sigh that broke through into her half-dreaming state. Then she heard Adham speak to the horse which immediately quivered, suddenly stopped. His arm eased her forward, away from the support of his body and from the protection of his cloak. As he swung himself on to the

159

ground, he spoke to her, then held up his arms so that she slid into them.

At the very moment when he reached for her, the wind sprang up with renewed ruthlessness so that the words he was shouting were at once tossed away from them. Cindy half-turned her back trying to protect herself from the fearful onslaught, and closing her eyes against the invading sand.

Apparently he decided that it was pointless to speak any more, instead he seized her arm and gripping it firmly propelled her forward. She had no idea where they were going but she had sufficient confidence to trust him completely. That he found what he was searching for was apparent when, a little time later, after stumbling in the direction he indicated, Cindy found herself, half-pushed, half-falling into a tiny crevice on the ground with behind her, sheltering her from the worst of the blast a little outcrop of rock.

Panic returned to her when she realised that she was alone again, that

Adham had disappeared but her dismay lasted only for a moment when she remembered that he had to make arrangements for the horse. It must have been ten minutes before he came back and by then Cindy was huddled against the rock, shivering a little as if she were cold, her arms wrapped round her body.

He did not speak when he came back but lowered himself on to the ground beside her. The torch was shone on her face, moving intimately from the top of her tangled head to the tips of her toes in their borrowed riding boots, before resting briefly on her face for an instant before being extinguished. Then, without being aware of the source of the comfort, she had the impression that something had come between herself and the wind, that she was no longer at the mercy of its more brutal whims.

It was like a dream when she realised that she was being covered again with the long cloak that he wore. That together they were being wrapped cocoon like in the huge soft folds. And

161

it was like a dream to find his arms about her. They lay together on the bare sand, she felt his hands move caressingly down over her shoulders, smoothing the thin silk of her blouse until they linked loosely round her waist.

With a sigh of content, she moved, moulding herself against the hard length of his body, her forehead nestling in the silky beard. It was with difficulty she resisted the temptation to raise her lips to his. He adjusted his position and she felt his arms tighten momentarily round her, heard him murmur something she couldn't understand.

Then, 'Rest now Lucinda.'

A smile touched her mouth, her hands spread out over the gentle rising and falling of the broad chest. And she wished, how she wished, that she could stay like this for ever.

★　★　★

The sun peeping over the horizon, shadows lengthening on the sands brought Cindy slowly to life. Before she opened her eyes she gave a contented little sigh and stretched carefully. Twice during the night she had wakened, longing to move her cramped position but each time, reluctant to disturb Adham, she had lain without moving until sleep had once more overtaken her.

But now, experimentally she twisted one wrist in an effort to relieve the tingling in her arm and to her surprise encountered no restricting presence, no comforting arms round her. She sat bolt upright, sweeping aside the cloak which had been tucked round her, ignoring the discomfort of various limbs which protested at her sudden move. In the faint morning light she could see that she was alone but a moment's reflection told her that Adham must be close at hand and had no doubt gone to assure himself that his horse was unharmed after the night's storms.

Recollection brought a faint shiver to

her body. Looking round she could see that the sand had been moulded into all kinds of weird shapes, drifted like snow into surrealistic sculptures. Even as she noticed that she became aware once more of the stinging residue of sand against her skin, in her hair and mouth.

With a sigh, she got up, shaking out the huge cloak, eyes closed against the grit which this action caused to fly around. So intent was she upon this that she failed to hear anyone approach.

His voice brought her whirling round to face him.

'So you are awake?' The green eyes sought and held hers. 'You slept well?'

At the sardonic note in his voice, Cindy felt the colour flare in her face. 'Yes.' Instinctively a hand went up to her head and her fingers confirmed what she had forgotten, that her hair must be an untidy mess. Again she faced him, attempting to subdue her agitation. She saw that his eyes were still red-rimmed but that his beard and hair were slightly damp so that he must have freshened up at the pool. As if in answer to an unspoken query and before she could say any more he spoke again.

'The water is cool and refreshing.' He paused, the green eyes noting, she was sure, every detail of her crumpled appearance. 'When you are ready, I think we should set out for home.' He turned away towards the horse which she could now see was tethered loosely to a palm tree about twenty yards from them.

It was bliss to lie face down cupping the water up over her face and neck. Her skin felt taut and painful but the water eased the discomfort so that when she stood up again she felt capable of dealing with whatever the day might bring. She had not failed to notice, when the green eyes had surveyed her so dominantly, a lurking spark which indicated that the last word had not been spoken on the foolhardiness of her exploit. The very idea brought a small shiver of fear, or perhaps it was excitement to her veins. Slowly, unaware that her damp shirt was clinging closely to her body, she went back to where she had slept. And Adham was waiting for her there, now looking more like a man of the desert than ever before, with the cloak that had sheltered them wrapped about him, leaving only the eyes clear.

He swung her up in front of the saddle with one easy movement and a moment later, he mounted behind her. Then they were riding across to the road, Cindy held strongly against his chest with his left hand while he controlled the horse with his right. The girl, remembering for the first time the disappearance of her own mount turned to him suddenly in an excess of anxiety.

'Oh, Hasa!' Her face was very close to his. 'I forgot about her until now.' There was pleading in her eyes as they looked into his. 'Tell me . . . '

For the first time there was the merest hint of a smile about the half-concealed mouth. 'Don't worry about it. Last night, when it was found that you weren't in your room, I was on my way to the stable when she came back.' He paused. 'And that fact did nothing to dispel my concern. As you can imagine,' he finished drily.

'I'm sorry.' Abruptly she turned from him, angered by the sting of tears which had unexpectedly affected her. Then hesitantly she looked round again. 'Not about the horse. I am so relieved about her. Last night I should have asked. But . . . '

'Yes, I know.' Surely she imagined that slight tightening of the arm that was round her waist. 'And perhaps I ought to have told you. But I was so relieved simply to find you — ' He broke off as if regretting that he had admitted so much. 'And in the middle of a sand-storm is not the best place to hold a rational conversation.'

By this time they had reached the perimeter of the grounds and the great stallion, as if in expectation of a good breakfast and disregarding the unaccustomed load, broke into a trot. When they reached the stables, Cindy was able to slide down from her somewhat uncomfortable position with a sense of relief. And if the Sheikh's assistance was rather more formal than she might have liked, then she put that down to the presence of the stable employees.

For they had come rushing out when they had heard the sound of their approach. First the stable boy, looking more than a little frightened and casting Cindy thought, a reproachful glance in her direction. She wondered if perhaps last night, when he had been so reluctant to saddle the horse for her, he had been trying to warn her that the weather conditions were liable to change.

Behind the boy, tall and stately, his robes flying out about him with the length of his stride, came Abdul. He spoke to his master, sliding one hand at the same time down the long highly bred nose of the stallion in a caressing gesture, but completely, and she thought deliberately, ignoring Cindy. Stubbornly, she went up to him, looking into the dark grizzled face.

'Hasa?' She spoke the mare's name slowly so that he was bound to understand. 'She is all right?'

The dark eyes turned reluctantly towards her, showing no hint of emotion or interest, he merely raised one hand, pointing in the direction of the stables.

'Thank you.' With her head high, the girl turned away and towards the door, aware that three pairs of eyes were following her. It was a relief to reach the shade of the interior, not only for the coolness beneath the whirring fans but more to escape what she felt was hostile scrutiny. With a longing for female companionship she hurried over to where Hasa was standing as calmly as ever and leaned her face against her flank. The mare, pausing in the act of chewing a mouthful of hay turned an untroubled head in her direction, surveyed the highly emotional girl for a moment before applying herself to the serious business of eating.

Cindy was walking along the corridor of the house, hoping to reach her room before she was overtaken, when she heard the long unmistakable stride behind her. A sense of panic rose inside her as the swish of his long robes sounded ever closer but she refused to look round.

Escape was almost within her grasp with the knob of the door turning, when one brown hand came out and covered hers. Feeling like a trapped animal she turned to face him but she didn't speak for she knew that if she did there was the danger that she would burst into undignified tears.

'Cindy. I have something to say to you.' He waited but when she did not answer he went on and there was a slight softening in his manner. 'But perhaps this is not the time. Later. First you will want a bath. And then we shall eat together. I shall be in the dining-room at eight o'clock as usual. And I shall expect to see you then.' And with that arrogant assumption, he swept off down the corridor.

8

She must have dropped off to sleep after her shower for the next thing she knew was a soft touch on her shoulder and she looked up into the smiling face of the girl who brought her tea in the morning. With a soft greeting, she indicated the tray before moving over to the window to pull the curtains.

The tea was refreshing. As she drank, Cindy moved a little stiffly, realising just how hard and comfortless the night in the desert had been. But at the time, she had scarcely noticed. Aware of a sweeping wave of emotion that she couldn't control, Cindy put down her cup with a bump, at the same time swinging her legs to the floor. She was due to appear on the carpet, she tried to laugh at herself, in less than half an hour, and the sooner she did something about her still damp hair, the better.

It was a very trim and businesslike young woman who walked along the corridor to the dining-room and certainly no one seeing her would have imagined that her heart was thumpting nervously. The dress she had chosen was in brown open-weave linen, the neckline trimmed with white and brown broderie anglais, cut in a simple style that skimmed her slender figure. Her feet were thrust into high heeled sandals and she had taken time to paint her toenails a soft dusty pink shade. As she pushed open the dining room door, she nervously put up a hand to push a lock of hair back beneath the broad white band which was holding her hair back from her face.

Adham turned from the window where he had been standing, a paper loosely held between his fingers. They looked at each other for a moment during which Cindy felt the increasing warmth in her cheeks. In an effort to appear at her ease she said, 'Good morning,' in what she realised was a particularly pert voice, quite unlike her normal tone. At once she saw his dark eyebrows come together but then they cleared and his voice as he answered was bland and amiable.

She sat down on the chair he held out for her, shaking out her napkin and facing him bravely when he took the seat opposite.

'Thank you.' He took the cup of coffee that she held out to him leaning back and stirring it, but with all his attention apparently focussed on his guest. Cindy tried to brace herself for what she was sure must follow. But when he spoke it was on an entirely different matter.

'My mother wishes that I should take you to visit Nevine. If you are free this morning, then we can drive into the city.'

'I have nothing else that I want to do.' She wiped some crumbs from her mouth with the napkin, before placing it back on the table. 'I have finished all my work. I don't imagine that the

Sheikha wants me to show the sketches to Nevine . . . '

'No. I think she will wish to make the decision herself. In fact, I'm not certain that my cousin knows the reason for your visit.' He paused. Then, 'You say you have finished your work?'

'Yes.' She forced her eyes from his and appeared to concentrate on the few crumbs on her plate. 'I told your mother that I would like to go back to London as soon as possible. Mr Gascoigne will be expecting me.'

'Then you must let me know when you would like me to book a flight. I expect my mother will be back tomorrow and then we can arrange it.'

Cindy was so shocked at the casual way he spoke, making no polite sounds of regret that her eyes shot open as she looked at him.

'Thank you.' She was furious with herself when she heard the slight tremble in her voice. The chair grated noisily on the polished floor as she pushed it back. Then, anger with herself made her continue, 'Am I allowed to go now?'

The Sheikh paused in the midst of lighting a cigar. Very slowly he waved his hand, extinguishing the lighted match, his eyes narrowed against the curl of smoke.

'Allowed to go, Miss Charles? What do you mean?' His tone sounded as sarcastic as she had intended her own to be.

'You said . . . Earlier you said that you had something to say to me . . . '

'Earlier?' There was a puzzled frown on his face which suddenly cleared. 'Oh . . . ' The white teeth shone in a flashing grin. 'Oh, you mean when we returned after our . . . our night together in the desert?'

Cindy felt the blush start in the soles of her feet and wash over her. It was all too evident that he noticed and enjoyed her discomfiture for he continued.

'Well, if you want to talk about it I suggest that you sit down again.' He waved vaguely to her chair and she sat down abruptly, more because her legs were weak than because of any inclination to do so. 'That's better.' He resumed his seat opposite, pushing aside his plate and cup and pulling a heavy crystal ashtray towards him.

'Now ... Last night ... I had decided that perhaps it was best to avoid the subject, especially when you indicated that you were more than ready to go back to England.'

'I didn't say that. At least,' she saw one disbelieving eyebrow go up, 'not in the rude way you implied.'

'Ah.' He stared at the glowing end of the cigar. 'Last night.' His voice hardened. 'Last night what you did was unbelievably fool-hardy. Dangerous not only to yourself but to others also.'

She felt a cold trickle run down her spine but all the same was reluctant to accept his censure. 'It did not seem so at the time. It was a perfectly clear night and you told me yourself that the desert was empty.'

There was a long pause before he

answered. 'It was not a perfectly clear night. I believe that Ahali tried to warn you . . . '

'Ahali?' She broke in. 'Do you mean the stable boy?'

'Yes.'

'I — I didn't understand. I thought he was telling me how late it was. But it was a beautiful night. The sky was so clear.'

'You should always believe an Arab when he tries to give advice about the weather. They can smell changes approaching, can sense the least little sign.'

'I'm — I'm sorry.'

'I'm sure you are.' There was coldness about him now. 'But because you were so foolish, disregarding all sensible convention, those who tried to help you are now in serious trouble.'

'Who? What? I don't understand.'

'Because he was the person who allowed you to get into such trouble, the boy is now in a very difficult position.'

Only the seriousness of his expression prevented her from laughing at the absurdity of what he had said. 'But he can't be blamed. Of course he can't. It was entirely my fault.' She shook her head impatiently. 'It was true what he said. He did try to tell me I ought not to go. Surely you — '

'It is not for me to interfere. Abdul is in charge of the stables. There his word is paramount.'

'But this is absurd.' Anxiety brought a sobbing laugh to the girl's throat. 'The boy was in no way responsible. Why should he be blamed?'

'Miss Charles. This is not Tottenham Court Road, you know . . . '

'Thank you.' She felt an unexpected flare of anger. 'I had noticed.'

'As I was saying, this is not London and you need not expect the same codes. Ahali has been judged, at least by Abdul, to have neglected his duties in allowing one of the guests of the family to run into danger.'

'Punish me if you like.' She could not

get the picture of the small pleading face from her mind and in her anger she thumped the table with a clenched fist. 'Punish me.'

'Perhaps that is your punishment.'

Uncomprehendingly she stared at him. Then she understood. 'Do you mean . . . ' Disbelief had made her voice tense and strained. 'Do you mean that the boy being punished, knowing the boy is being punished, is the price I have to pay?'

The hand holding the half-smoked cigar suddenly crushed it out in a violent gesture. 'That is what I meant.' His voice was weary.

'But that is inhuman, isn't it?' she pleaded. And when he didn't answer, again, 'Isn't it? Look,' impulsively she extended her hands towards him in a pleading gesture, 'if I ask you . . . If I beg you . . . to make it all right. After all, you must be able to do something, your word means something.' With the emotion she felt, her voice rose a little. 'You are the Sheikh.'

Almost in anger he pushed back his chair and strode to the window. 'I told you . . . ' There was bleakness in his voice. 'I told you that the title means nothing. It is a mere formality, a polite form of address.' He turned round to look at her but she was too involved in her own feelings at that moment to see the air of strain about his eyes and mouth.

Her legs were trembling as she stood up but her voice was curiously flat. 'You mean you won't do anything. Then if you won't,' she turned away to walk to the door, 'I shall have to try to think what I can do myself.'

But before she could leave the room, she felt herself being caught by the arm and turned roughly back to face him. 'You will not interfere, do you hear me?' His voice was hard and dictatorial, the green eyes searched hers, trying to impose his will. 'Do you hear me, Cindy?' he repeated when she did not answer, giving her a little shake.

But the sound of her name on his

lips, spoken even in a voice as unfriendly as the one he had used undermined all the courage she had found in the last few minutes. That and the touch of his hands on her arms, a touch that sent the blood coursing wildly through her veins, reminded her of the night she had spent in his arms. To her dismay she felt a sob rise in her throat, heard it burst from her lips.

'Cindy.' Again he shook her but this time gently. And his voice was milder, tender even, his hands slid down her arms, lingered about her wrists. 'Cindy.' Gently he pulled her against him, one hand beneath her chin tilting her face to his. For a wild and breathless minute she imagined that he was going to kiss her, her heart seemed to melt in expectation of it. But just then, outside the door, they heard a soft footstep as the maid came from the kitchen to clear the table and the moment, the possibility faded, his arms dropped and he turned away.

When he spoke, his voice was

business-like and matter-of-fact.

'I have one or two telephone calls to make, Cindy. I shall be ready to leave in about half-an-hour. If that will suit you.'

★   ★   ★

'You will be pleased to know . . . '

At the sound of his voice, she turned her attention from the road to look at him, reflecting that with the concealing dark glasses and the habitual white robes, driving the almost obligatory large Mercedes sports car, there was nothing the least bit English about him. He had all the accoutrements, all the appearance of the average oil-rich sheikh, a bit younger than many perhaps, more handsome certainly but fairly typical just the same. Bleakly she returned her attention to the road, noticing how he slowed to pass a group of camels with their riders. That at least wasn't typical, she thought. Most drivers simply hooted loudly, put a foot

183

down and sliced on.

'Yes?' Almost without interest she waited for him to continue what he had been saying.

'You will be pleased to know that I've put that matter . . . right.'

Her head shot round. 'You mean . . . ' She felt her spirits rise in a crazily optimistic arc.

'Yes.' His head turned and he grinned briefly. The world seemed to swing round her. 'I have told Abdul that on this occasion it was not Ahali's fault. I have told him that our visitor has led a peculiarly emancipated life, away from the restraints of firm parental control, living with a group of young people in college rooms and now alone in London.'

'I see.' Her voice was drily amused.

'Yes. He understood. And he shook his head in wonder. He appeared to think in the end, that it was a miracle that you had survived as long as you had.' He negotiated a set of traffic lights skilfully avoiding a wobbling motor cyclist. 'In the end he gave it as his opinion that the only thing that would settle you down would be if you could find a husband. Only, he didn't think it would be too easy.'

Cindy wasn't certain whether she was being teased or not but as she turned to look out of the side window, she felt her lips twitch. 'And did you agree with him?'

'About what?' He swung the car into the street where his cousin lived. 'Oh, you mean about the difficulty of finding a husband who would be prepared to accept such a provoking independent woman? Oh, I think Abdul imagines that I share his views. But in fact . . . ' he turned the car into the shady court-yard, ' . . . I don't think you'll have the slightest difficulty.' He switched off the engine, sat staring ahead. 'You are how old Cindy?' As if unaware of what he was doing he raised one of her hands to his cheek. The silky hairs of his beard trembled against her skin. 'Twenty? Twenty-one?' Unexpectedly he turned to scrutinise her.

'I'm . . . I'm twenty-two.' She pulled her hand from his, pretending to search in her handbag for something.

'And still no sign of a husband?' he asked mockingly. Then, as she did not reply, 'But perhaps I'm wrong. I'm sure that young man at the airport has every intention of rectifying that situation.'

'That's nonsense. I told you so at the time.' Irritation made her short.

'Oh, I don't know.' He appeared to consider the situation. 'I thought I discerned certain proprietorial signs.'

'A kiss?' Cindy decided to be amused. 'You know we are living in the twentieth century. In England at least.' And satisfied that she had got the last word, she pushed open the door of the car.

Her second visit to Nevine was less difficult than the first, probably because she knew what to expect. Understanding more, she had brought with her a scarf to cover her hair, sparing the feelings of the servant who opened the door for them. She even clutched it across her face when she thought he was about to turn to look at her and pulled her loose jacket more tightly about her in case he should catch a glimpse of her arms. As they followed him across the hall, Cindy sensed an amused glance from Adham but she refused to respond.

Nevine appeared to be genuinely pleased to see them, coming from behind her open work screen when she had ascertained that the male visitor was indeed her cousin. They spoke to each other in Arabic before Nevine turned to greet Cindy.

'How kind of you to come and see me again.' Cindy saw the red lips move in a smile.

'I was very pleased to come. I should not have liked to go back to England without seeing you again.'

During the visit, they drank sherbet and ate the sticky sweet-meats which Cindy had encountered on her first visit. She was glad that the girl appeared to enjoy Adham's company, laughing at his teasing and showing none of the reserve that might have been expected. But still, watching the girl, seeing how she had to lift aside the barqa each time she raised the glass to her lips, Cindy couldn't quite subdue the *frisson* of horror that she had experienced on her first visit.

How she wondered, how on earth could a woman who had been brought up in such a cloistered way ever be happy in an intimate relationship with a man? To her it seemed as unnatural as the life of an anchorite nun must have been.

After about an hour Cindy saw Adham glance at his watch and by then she herself was more than ready to go. Although she had found it quite an experience coming in contact with such an unusual style of living, she found it sad and depressing and the effort of trying to adapt her conversation to the situation was a strain.

As they drove away from the house, towards the shopping area of the town which Adham had suggested she might like to visit, Cindy was quiet, intensely occupied with her own thoughts and some inner turmoil.

'What are you thinking of?' He had driven the car into a private garage and turned to face her. There was something about his watchful look behind the dark glasses that told her he understood only too well what had caused the slight dejection. 'You seem . . . withdrawn.'

'Of course not,' she denied firmly, looking away from him and towards a chattering group of women who were walking towards their car. The chauffeur sprang out to relieve them of their parcels and to bow them into their seats. 'It just seems so sad . . . ' The words were out almost before she realised she had spoken. Certainly it had not been her intention to discuss Nevine's position with him. Apologetically she faced him again. 'I'm sorry. It's none of my business, I know.'

To her surprise he smiled. 'Would it

surprise you to know that Nevine is perfectly happy with her lot?'

'But that's not the point.' The words once again burst from her impulsively.

'Isn't it?' The smile had faded. 'I should have thought that it was very much the point.'

'But she doesn't know . . . '

'Doesn't know? Of course she knows. Nevine is a very intelligent educated young woman. Oh, she never went to school or university perhaps, but she had the finest teachers, she speaks and reads several languages. Would it offend you to know that she feels the same sorrow over your situation that you feel for hers?'

Cindy stared up at him. 'But that is ridiculous!'

'Ridiculous. Absurd.' His voice hardened a little. 'You use such words too casually when speaking of things you don't understand.' Behind the dark glasses, his eyes seemed to glare. Then relenting a little, he spoke in a gentler voice, reflectively, as if trying to assure himself of something as well as his guest. 'Believe me, the most difficult thing is to try to reconcile the opposing cultures. My cousin seems to me to have chosen very wisely. For her, life is simple and straightforward, with none of the complications — '

He broke off suddenly and sat for a moment without speaking. The only sound was the gentle hum of the car's air-conditioning. Then with a laugh, he reached out a hand to touch hers. 'But we must not become too serious. Are you ready to brave the oven outside? Shall we make a dash for the nearest department store?' Without waiting for her reply, he got out of the car and held the door for her. 'And then,' he continued, as he led the way in the direction of the street, 'tonight I have accepted an invitation on your behalf. Tonight,' he paused as they reached the bustling throng that surged along the main shopping street, 'tonight some friends have invited us to eat dinner with them in the desert. In the true Bedu style.'

9

In spite of what her wild imaginings had told her, Cindy found herself being driven to the party in the same luxurious car which had taken them into town. She had teased herself with the idea that they might be required to go by camel. After all, if it was to be, as Adham had explained, a party given for several important western business men, probably the host wanted to lay on the whole Arabian scene, with guests arriving, like stars in some fabulous film scenario, in the most dramatic manner possible.

It had been pleasant to lie in the scented green water of her bath, planning it all in her mind's eye. There would be the dark velvet sky, a full moon dropping down behind the few palm trees and across the horizon would come three, four, five camels, walking with that strange rolling gait up to the large tent, softly lighted from the inside . . .

Yes, she supposed that kind of Arabia did still exist. As well as the streets filled with expensive cars, the air-conditioned stores selling everything from tumble driers to plastic picnic cups, from silks at a hundred dollars a metre to electric fires complete with coal-effect dog grates and teak surrounds.

She, confident with Adham as her guide, had been more interested in the small local bazaars selling a variety of goods which had at least some connection with the area. And although her escort, amused at her pleasure in the simple open-fronted shops assured her that even the apparently local goods were mostly imported, it was on these that Cindy concentrated for the few presents she wanted to take home with her.

On the whole Adham had allowed her to go ahead with her own bargaining, watching with amusement as she sought the best terms. Once or twice, he made some interjection causing the shopkeeper to shrug, protest and then agree to the price that she, in sign language and broken English was suggesting. She was grateful for his protection, knowing that alone she would never have dared to venture so far from the bigger European style shops. And in the main she was very pleased with the purchases she had made. A small prayer mat for Marjorie, something that would look bright and cheerful on a plain white wall, a little stool, carved from what Adham told her was carob wood and several plates from the same wood.

It had been mid-afternoon before they had finished and by then they were tired and glad to make their way to the world-famous hotel for a meal. When she went into the large foyer, Cindy was reminded of that day when the adventure had all begun, that day when she had been summoned to the London hotel to see the Sheikha. She recalled her disappointment when all she had seen of Adham was his back disappearing in the direction of the lifts.

'What are you thinking of?' he had asked for the second time that day.

'Oh, nothing.' The same reply as before. But she had blushed and looked down at her plate.

★   ★   ★

But now, speeding along dusty desert roads Adham at the wheel of the car, she felt a strange mixture of content and excitement. Content because she was with him and knowing there could be little else between them, that was almost for the moment enough. And excitement because of that look she had surprised when she had walked through from her bedroom to join him. She had worn the dress that the previous night she had discarded with such passionate disappointment.

Of course it had been a wild extravagance. But with the open cheque she had been given by the firm to buy whatever she required, she had been able to stifle her conscience. And the saleswoman in the small exclusive boutique where she had bought it, sensing her shock at the price tag had offered to knock five per cent from the bill.

And now she had no regrets. The dress was as demure as anything even the most conservative Arab could require. The balloon sleeves came down to the wrist where they were gathered into slender cuffs and the high neckline with the small mandarin collar was modesty itself. All the beauty of the dress was concentrated in the silk and skilful cut which moulded the material to her shapely figure, hugging the slender waist before flaring out in a skirt which swirled round her ankles when she walked.

And the colours, a mixture of sea greens and jade which altered according to the light and movement, emphasised the girl's unusual fairness.

Then to complete the ensemble, what better choice than the jewellery she had been wearing that very first night? The slender gilt chain and pendant consisting of a knot of intricately woven strands, the sophisticated earrings shown to more advantage tonight since she had decided to wear her hair on top of her head, were the perfect finishing touch to the perfect dress.

★　★　★

'Have we far to go?' It seemed such a long time since they had spoken, she wondered if he had the same awareness as she was experiencing. When she had appeared from her bedroom half an hour earlier, something electric had sprung into life between them. And walking along the corridor together, she had caught sight of them both in a mirror, was immediately struck how each seemed a foil for the other. Both tall, but his darkness stressing her own fairness, his white robes complementing her dazzling dress, his simplicity saying something about her fashionable Western appearance. But that thought which could have been depressing only increased the sense of tantalising expectation she was experiencing.

'Not far now.' When he spoke she felt his glance flick over her. 'Are you tired?'

There was a special note in his voice that brought her face up to look at him. 'Tired?' The moonlight played on the cheekbones, glittered in the eyes now intent on the road. 'Of course I'm not tired. Why should I be? I slept for an hour after we got home . . . ' And then she remembered last night and thought she understood what he was speaking of. Her cheeks burned and she hastily turned from him to look through the side window of the car. 'No.' Her voice was perfectly calm. 'I don't feel in the least tired.'

'Good.' The monosyllable might have been abrupt but for the gentleness of his voice. And after a moment he continued. 'Then we need not worry about leaving and can wait as late as you wish. I thought that perhaps — '

He broke off. 'My mother will be returning about four in the morning, but I expect she will be staying the night in Riyadh. She usually stays at the airport hotel when she arrives during the night. It is so much more convenient.' He swung the car off the metalled road, on to a dirt track which meandered alongside what appeared to be a dried up river bed. The Sheikh explained casually, pointing briefly to the sweep of white shingle topped by flat boulders.

'The bed of an ancient wadi.' He paused while he negotiated a deep pothole in the road, picking up speed as the road climbed slightly until they reached a point where they could look down on the dry ravine. 'The bed of the Great Wadi lies beneath our feet, a long way down. The oases in this area are simply where the waters burst through the earth's crust and reach the surface.'

'But why . . . If they know the water's

there, why don't they bring it to the surface?'

'No one's found an economic way to do it yet.'

'But what do economics matter to a country as rich as this?'

'But they do.' There was an amused tolerant tone in his voice as he spoke to her. 'I don't think there's a country in the world where they don't.'

'But the Saudis have so much money.'

'Yes, and they spend a lot. Do you know that the hospital in Riyadh is almost the most up-to-date and well-equipped in the world?'

'I can imagine. But that doesn't alter the fact that the people are still very poor.'

'No. You're right, of course. And you're right in thinking that the only thing that is going to improve matters generally is if they can find water. In large quantities.' Suddenly he pointed towards where there was a faint luminosity some distance ahead of them. 'There. Can you see? A Bedu camp.' And for some reason she could not understand, he laughed rather bitterly.

Cindy had had no idea what to expect although when he had spoken of the party, Adham had given the impression that it could be a fairly sophisticated affair. Vaguely she had thought that there might be a rather large tent and possibly some evidence of cooking outside. In fact if she thought of it at all seriously, what came into her mind was a rather grand barbecue in the desert.

In fact the sight that greeted them was much more lavish and spectacular than any that one would have expected outside the set of a film of the Queen of Sheba. They left the car a short distance from the camp beside the dozen or so others that had been parked in the special area provided, and walked along the dark blue carpet that had been laid over a foundation of flat stones.

'Am I dreaming?' The words sprang

unbidden to Cindy's lips, her pulses raced at the sound of his deep intimate laughter, followed by the guiding touch of his hand on her elbow.

'I'm not surprised that you should think so. I almost did, too, when I first saw the set-up. But Nazir has always had more than his fair share of showmanship. And it impresses the visitors.' There was a hint of cynicism in his manner. 'As you said . . . Perhaps the Arabs have their priorities wrong.'

'But I didn't . . . ' she protested then stopped, the words stifled by the full melodrama of the scene that was now fully revealed.

The tent, hugely wide, billowing slightly with some hidden artificial source of draught, was made of a dark silky material which allowed the lights to filter through from the inside. To the right and behind the tent, were two long low buildings which at least in appearance owed nothing to the twentieth century, being so far as Cindy could discern in the moonlight, some kind of wooden frame 'thatched' with palm fronds and with some kind of hanging cloth for doorways. As they watched, several times, the drapes were pushed aside and men could be seen entering and leaving.

To one side of the tent, was the part that nature had laid on specially for such occasions, the oasis, this time heavily fringed with date palms and even a group of camels standing silently against the skyline. It was so perfect that it was almost unbearable. She caught her breath and as his hand touched hers, the fingers closed about each other.

'Come and meet Nazir.' His voice was low and intimate even if the words were not the ones she would have liked to hear him speak. But willingly enough she allowed herself to be led forward to the looped-back entrance and through the silken inside curtains.

No sooner had they stepped through the concealing folds than their host came forward to welcome them. His greeting to Adham was the typical rather charming Arab one of a touch to the chest and then to the forehead but when he turned to her, Nazir held out his hand in the formal western manner.

'Miss Charles. It is such a pleasure to meet you.' The liquid dark eyes were blatantly admiring. 'I am glad that Adham was able to bring you.' His English was as faultless as Adham's. 'And now, I would like you to meet my wife.' He turned towards a group behind them and a small woman, dressed in a gold lamé trouser suit detached herself and came forward holding out both hands to Adham. It gave Cindy a pang to see him take them, pull the woman towards him and kiss her on both cheeks.

'Adham. It's been such ages.' The voice was low and throaty with a quite distinct American deep south accent. The smiling face turned to Cindy. 'Hello, honey. Welcome to the greatest show on earth.'

'Thank you.' She felt that she was

hiding her surprise skilfully. 'It was kind of you to ask me.'

'Think nothing of it. I was so pleased when Nazir told me that we would be having an English girl tonight. The others,' she spoke in a not particularly low voice, waving in the direction of the group of people she had just left, 'are mostly German and Dutch. What did you say your name was?'

'It's Cindy Charles.'

'Well, I'm Betty.' As she spoke, Betty pulled one of Cindy's hands through her arm and began to introduce her to the others. As she had said, they were mainly Europeans, but there were two Arabs apart from Adham and Nazir and both of them had brought their wives with them.

After a bit of general conversation, Cindy found herself speaking to one of the Saudi women, a young and shy pretty girl, dressed in the height of Paris fashion but looking pathetically uncomfortable in this international gathering. At first it was a bit difficult to find a topic that interested both of them but by sheerest luck Cindy mentioned that she had been to visit Adham's cousin and Maryam's face lit up.

'Do you mean Nevine? Oh, how I wish I had seen her. But we, my husband and I, have been abroad for six months and have just returned.' The pretty face darkened, there was a little sigh. 'How I have missed seeing her.'

'Then I imagine she will be very pleased to see you. You are close friends?'

'Yes. I used to take lessons with her. Of course,' a faint smile lightened the gloomy expression, 'she was always much brighter than I. Our teacher used to berate me a little for being so much lazier than Nevine. But . . . they were such happy times.' The smile faded, almost as if happy times had gone from her life for ever.

'Yes.' Cindy answered rather uncertainly. 'Schooldays often seem happy when one looks back. But for myself, I must say I was itching to leave when I was eighteen.'

'Of course, school would be different. But Nevine and I had lessons in her home. We were taught by an English-woman who was married to a French diplomat. No, it isn't so much that I miss the lessons. Only . . . ' she hesitated as if reluctant to speak, 'only life was so much simpler.' A faint colour stained her cheeks and then in a rush, as if afraid she might change her mind. 'I don't really think I suit this life. But Khalil wishes me to go with him when he travels and I must do what he wants.'

'But surely,' Cindy began gently, 'if you explain, tell him that you'd rather stay at home . . . '

'Oh, I couldn't possibly do that. You see — ' She broke off suddenly, looking confused, almost frightened and began feverishly to talk about her recent visit to America. 'Yes, New York is the most exciting city, especially when you first see it from the air.'

'Oh. My mother lives in New York.' Cindy looked up at the tall figure who now joined them. She saw how the shining dark eyes glanced quickly from Maryam to herself then back to the Arab girl.

'This is my husband, Miss Charles.' There was a flicker of anxiety in the girl's eyes as she made the cursory introduction. 'We have been talking about New York. Miss Charles' mother lives there.'

'Indeed.' The intense gaze appraised the tall fair girl. 'And you have come with Adham, have you not?'

'Yes. She is with me.' To Cindy's great relief, she felt Adham touch her arm, saw Khalil's eye note the intimacy of the gesture. Somehow, without being told she knew that the two men did not care for each other. 'Maryam.' Adham turned to the girl. 'I am pleased to see you after so long. Have you been to visit Nevine?'

'No.' As the girl smiled and shook her head, Cindy noticed that she cast a slightly apprehensive glance at her husband. 'But I hope to go soon. Please tell her so.'

'I shall.' There was an unusual gentleness in the way he replied. Then, 'You will know of course that she is being married soon.'

'No, I did not know.'

'Yes. She is to marry the eldest son of Sharif Shakir.'

'I am glad. Please tell her.'

'I will tell her.'

Then Cindy found herself being guided in the direction of two newcomers. She was introduced to them and took one of the glasses of champagne that were being handed round. She didn't take much part in the conversation, being content to listen and to absorb the atmosphere.

Inside the tent was as exotic and unexpected as the outside setting had been. The floor was strewn with what appeared to be priceless oriental carpets, their rich colours immediately catching the eye and setting the scene. Round the walls were divans, piled with cushions dark red with gold cords and tassels, low tables of polished brass on which burned small lamps with ruby shades and casting a flattering glow.

Cindy found herself sitting on one of the divans, listening to something that one of the Dutchmen was trying to tell her. Although his English was as perfect as everyone else's she was having difficulty in understanding, perhaps because her attention was diverted by the intense conversation Adham was having with his hostess. Betty was laughing vivaciously up into his face and Adham had thrown back his head in amusement.

'So you see,' the Dutchman allowed his hand to rest on hers, 'when one travels as much as I do, then inevitably the marriage suffers.'

'Yes.' Abstractedly the girl removed her hand from the slightly clammy touch. Then, trying to give her attention to her companion, 'But can't your wife come with you?'

'But that is just what I have been telling you.' He sounded a little aggrieved. 'My wife and I separated last year.' Again his hand came out, this time playfully pulling her fingers. 'And that is why I get so much consolation from the company of a pretty girl like you.'

'Oh dear.' Cindy only half-heard, her attention again being drawn to the couple who stood so intimately together just a few yards from them.

'Oh, I see how it is.' A slightly sneering note in the Dutchman's voice this time succeeded in capturing her entire attention. She saw the blue eyes in the fattish face slide meaningfully towards Adham and back to herself. 'I see.' He repeated. 'The green eyed monster is about.' He sighed heavily. 'Well, I don't suppose we ordinary businessmen can get a look in when the oil-rich sheikhs are available. But, if I were you my dear,' he leaned towards her as if he were in danger of being overheard, 'I should be very careful. I have heard that they treat their women in a very peculiar way.' There was a little unpleasant laugh. 'Things that I wouldn't care to discuss with an innocent girl like you.' He put an emphasis on that last part that made Cindy's cheeks flare. Abruptly she stood up.

'Thank you for telling me.' Then with a sudden inspiration she leaned towards him confidentially. 'I should be careful,' she said softly, 'I've heard that they can treat guests in a very peculiar way. Especially those who trespass on their hospitality.'

Holding her empty glass in one hand, she walked over to where Adham was still standing with Betty. She couldn't hear what they were talking about but as she came near, he looked up and their eyes met unexpectedly. There was something in his expression, as if for a moment it was unguarded, that made her heart swing giddily. Neither of them was aware that Betty, noticing that she had lost his attention, followed the direction of his eyes, before with a smiling shrug moving away from them, to a group of the other guests.

The only thing that Cindy was conscious of was Adham. And she knew in that shattering instant what she had been trying to conceal from herself since they had met. What she had thought of as a silly rather juvenile infatuation was much more than that. She loved him with a quite desperate longing. And knowing that between them love was impossible would have no effect on her feelings whatsoever.

10

'You would like another drink, Cindy?'

'What?' She started a little when he took the glass that she had been holding and as they looked at each other again, she wondered if, beneath the tan he had lost a little colour. But the idea was so absurd that she dismissed it instantly. It was an effort to smile but she did so, wondering at her ability to deceive.

'Yes, if I may.' She watched him turn, raise a hand to one of the servants who at once came across with the glasses set out on a silver tray. She took one, raising it to her lips, but noticing that the glass he had selected held a colourless effervescent liquid. 'I was surprised to be offered champagne.' She was determined to speak normally, determined that he should know nothing of what she was feeling. 'I thought alcohol was forbidden.'

'For Moslems it is.' He sipped thoughtfully. 'But so long as it isn't flaunted too publicly then a blind eye is turned to what foreigners drink.'

'And you?' She jerked a hand in the direction of his glass. 'I don't think that's champagne.'

'No. This is tonic water.'

'Oh.' That seemed to confirm that he adhered pretty closely to the dictates of his religion. The thought had a depressing effect and in an attempt to counteract this, she drained her glass.

He gave the impression of being locked in his own thoughts. And those, judging from his expression gave him no great pleasure. Moodily he looked away from her and she sensed relief when they were joined by some of the other guests.

The rest of the evening passed in a haze and later Cindy wondered if perhaps she had had too many glasses of champagne. Certainly it developed into a fairly noisy evening, all of the

215

guests determinedly enjoying themselves. The meal which was served
about ten was, so they were assured by
Nazir simple Bedu fare, but it was hard
to imagine that the desert nomads
dined so well.

The main course consisted of rice,
set out on huge platters and a stew
made of mutton, and rich with the
scent of herbs. Cindy was surprised to
find it quite delicious, not at all the
rather greasy tough meal she might
have expected. Betty, despite her
husband's rather half-hearted remonstrance insisted that their guests should
be given spoons and forks to eat with so
at least they were not obliged totally to
conform to local custom. After the meat
they were offered sticky, very sweet
cakes, then figs, dates and other fruits.
Finally they drank tiny cups of the
powerful coffee that seemed to be the
preferred taste in the Middle East with
pieces of Turkish Delight.

Throughout the meal the champagne
flowed freely and Cindy suspected that

she was not the only one who had drunk too much. In any case, the food and wine had the effect of making her eyelids droop so that she was relieved when Adham, after murmuring in her ear and receiving her consent suggested that it was time to leave.

Unexpectedly she shivered a little as she waited for Adham to complete his goodbyes. How strange on such a sultry warm night. Even in the tent with fans directing a cooling draught over huge concealed blocks of ice, it had been warm and humid.

'Why are you shivering? Are you perhaps frightened?' It was the Dutchman again, his face florid, his manner insinuating.

'Frightened?' Cindy smiled discouragingly. 'What do you mean?'

'Oh, I thought maybe you had considered what I said and decided that you were playing with fire.'

Impatiently Cindy turned away from him, not troubling to reply but the Dutchman had the last word.

'There's nothing money can't buy, is there? I imagine those trinkets you are wearing are worth a pretty penny.'

It was with relief that Cindy saw Adham coming towards them, he cast a swift glance from her face to the man, nodded rather distantly to him, then, putting a hand on her elbow, led her out into the night.

The journey home began in silence but before they had gone very far, the headlamps cutting through the now dark night, he spoke quite casually.

'Well, what did you think of it?'

'It was wonderful. Very interesting. Thank you for taking me.' How formal and stilted, she thought.

'You met someone you liked? A Dutchman was he not?'

'I didn't like him.' Anger and disappointment flared through her in a searing wave.

'Oh? I got the impression . . . ' He considered for a moment. 'May I ask why you didn't like him?'

'No reason.' Of course she couldn't

tell him what had been insinuated. 'You know how it is. Some people you like on sight. Others . . . well.'

'Mmm.' He was silent for a bit. Then, 'Did you know that Maryam and Nevine are . . . were, I suppose I ought to say . . . great friends?'

'Yes, she told me.' Cindy turned in her seat to look at him. 'I got the impression that she was unhappy.'

'I think it's likely. Unfortunately she married against her father's wishes. She has very doting parents; she is an only child and they agreed to her marriage only with the greatest reluctance. They are very devout Moslems, as Nevine's parents were, and Khalil is a very modern westernised young man. She happened to see him and decided that she would marry no one else. Her parents in the end gave in, which may not have been a good thing.'

'You only say that because she isn't happy. But if she had been, then naturally you would have taken the opposite view.'

'But surely the point *is* her unhappiness. Oh, I'm not fool enough to think that all arranged marriages are happy. All I'm saying is that for girls brought up as she was, as Nevine was, then perhaps they are unable to cope with the kind of life that you know. Just as,' and he spoke so carefully that Cindy felt that he was anxious that she should understand completely, 'just as you would find it difficult to fit into Nevine's situation.'

She had no difficulty in recognising what he was telling her and his message was so painful that she wanted to dispute what he was saying. 'But what about Betty? She and Nazir seem to be totally happy.'

There was a long pause during which Cindy sat with fast beating heart, watching blindly as he negotiated a number of sharp bends. At last, when they had reached a long straight road, he answered but slowly and Cindy thought, reluctantly.

'Nazir and Betty. But that is a different story.'

'Because it doesn't suit your argument?' Her unhappiness made her sound sharp, almost waspish.

'No, I wasn't thinking of that. Merely that . . . Betty is rather unusual. Probably the fact that she comes from the Southern States . . . '

'Does that mean she knows her place?'

But he seemed determined to ignore her sarcasm. 'No.' He spoke mildly. 'Not exactly. Although historically, perhaps there is something in what you say. No, when I said she was unusual, I meant that she is content to accept what might be a difficult position for a western woman, taking second place to Nazir's first wife, knowing that any children she has will not have the same place as his sons . . . '

'Oh. Do you — do you mean that he has two wives?'

'Not quite. At least, not at the same time. No, he divorced the mother of his sons in order to marry Betty. And I know that with her he is happier than he ever was before. But . . . He still looks after Samira, visits her regularly. And of course Betty is excluded from any of the family celebrations.'

'Yes, I see.' All at once Cindy felt particularly hopeless and disinclined to discuss the matter further. Stolidly she stared through the side window, watching the dim shapes slipping swiftly into the darkness. Then, almost without realising she was speaking, she voiced the last question she had in her mind.

'I understand why Maryam wanted to marry Khalil, obviously she fell in love with him. But I should have thought, if what you say about him is true, that she would have been the last kind he wished to marry.'

'Oh, did I forget to say? Of course, like many of such marriages, money was at the root of it. Maryam's family was very rich, while Khalil was poor and just beginning to make his way.'

'Well, it's no crime to be poor.'

When he didn't answer she could only conclude that he didn't agree with her. Resentful, she sat until the car turned into the courtyard and scarcely waited until it had pulled up in front of the house before she opened the door and began to hurry across the courtyard. About her, the night was dark as mourning, soft as silk, tempting her to hesitate for a moment before going indoors. And that moment was sufficient for him to overtake her, to open the door for her, gently to touch her hand. In short to do all those things which her subconscious demanded, which she was too proud to admit to herself.

Inside the hall, dimly lit as it was with pink shaded lamps, they faced each other and Cindy knew only the urgent longing to be folded into his arms, held strongly against that wide chest. A trickle of wildness ran through her as his fingers linked in hers, pulling her closer to him.

'Cindy.' The very sound of her name on his lips roused emotions which by their nature would be difficult to control. Her breath quickened, her heart throbbed in loud echoing beats which she knew must be obvious to him through the thin material of her dress. Inexorably his hands moved up her arms, tingling little movements that brought the blood singing into her veins until they reached her throat and stopped. Stopped but for that slight feathery touch, caressing, sensuous.

Her legs were too weak to move although one part of her brain told her that now was the time to fly. Vaguely she remembered what the Dutchman had hinted but it was too late for her to heed any advice that she had been given. She stared up into his eyes, those eyes which had cast their spell at the very first meeting. If they had been dark, she thought in tender despair, if they had been dark like any other Arab's, then she would never have given him another thought. And tonight she could have been out with someone ordinary like Jamie. But even if she tried she couldn't remember what

Jamie looked like. And she tried for a split second, until one of Adham's hands cupped the nape of her neck, the other circled her waist, pulling her irresistibly against him.

His mouth against hers was tender, tantalising, pulling her into a wild vortex that she hadn't known existed. With a shuddering little moan of surrender, she wound her arms round his neck, arched her body against his with seductive, thoughtless candour. His strengthening grasp, his more demanding mouth filled her with exultation, told her that his involvement was as great as her own.

'You know there is only one way this will end . . . ' His mouth had been on her closed lids, had moved tantalisingly along her temple. 'Is that what you want, Cindy?'

'Yes.' Desire had made her languorous, she slid her hands round and inside his robes, spreading her fingers across the rapidly beating heart, rejoicing in this unexpected power. 'Oh, yes.'

She released her breath in a shuddering sigh.

'You know what you are saying?' His mouth teased the lobe of her ear.

She was so bemused that she had no idea what she was saying, what she was agreeing to. All that she was aware of was that she longed to be like this for ever, held close to his chest. It was a moment before she sensed a slight withdrawal and her reaction to it was slow as the earlier one had been swift. She held back her head, smiling faintly, the hair which earlier had been elegantly piled at the back of her head now tumbled.

'Adham?' The pupils of her eyes dilated as the light caught them. 'Adham?' And now there was a hint of panic as she saw his expression.

'You are tired, Cindy. I should have remembered last night and made allowances for you.'

'Made allowances. For me?' If there was anguish in her voice he seemed to be unaware of it. 'Last night?' Then like a bolt she remembered how she had spent last night in his arms. Abruptly she pulled herself away, determined to hide the pain she was feeling.

'Of course you are right. I am tired.' She gave a sharp little laugh. 'And you must remember just how much champagne I have been drinking. I'm not used to it.' She put an expressive hand to her head. 'At least you can't blame alcohol for such foolishness.' She turned abruptly from him. 'Then I'll say goodnight, Adham.' She was pleased that her voice was so normal and she walked away, disregarding his attempt to detain her.

The door of her bedroom might have been banged loudly if it hadn't been for the hopelessness she felt. It was a gnawing pain in her chest; vaguely she wondered if a coronary felt like this. She undid the long zip at the back of her dress, letting it slip from her shoulders to lie in a pool on the carpet.

With a sigh, she walked over and sat down in front of the dressing table mirror, dispassionately admiring the slender green underskirt which was part of the dress. It was of a matching colour and round the bust was heavily trimmed with lace. She unpinned her untidy hair and began to brush with long steady strokes, smoothing out the tangles with a tearful impatience. The knock that sounded unexpectedly on the door made her pause, caused her heart to race treacherously. Before she could find breath to reply, another knock came, more imperious this time and Adham called her name.

She had no normal wish to see him. And she longed to see him. 'Yes? What is it?'

'May I come in?'

'Yes.' She looked round for her wrap but before she could move the door had opened and Adham was standing looking down at her.

'Cindy.' His gentleness was hard to bear. It would have been easier if he had been harsh. 'You seemed upset.'

'Of course I'm not.' She turned

round and began brushing her hair again. 'Only I'm tired, as you reminded me. And I'm longing to go to bed.'

'I understand.' From the way his eyebrows drew together she knew that she had annoyed him. 'Then I shan't keep you. I merely wanted to give you this.' And he held out a box, a blue box with gold lettering embossed on the lid. A box which she knew only too well for it was one of those which Daubeny and Gascoigne used every day to present their most exclusive jewellery. He put it down on the white top of the dressing-table and almost reluctantly she picked it up.

Before she pressed the tiny gold button she knew what it contained. And then when the lid flew open, the gleam of white metal and diamonds dazzled. Lying in their blue velvet cocoon, they flashed white fire. For a moment she stared at them, then with a decisive click she snapped the box shut, returning it to the dressing-table.

'I told your mother when she was in

London that I couldn't accept such expensive gifts.'

'I agree with you. It was a mistake then to offer such a gift, but surely things have changed now, Cindy.' In the glass he smiled down at her. 'Then we didn't know each other.'

'And now . . . Do we know each other so well?' Rising as she spoke she faced him mockingly, wondering even as she did so, where she got her courage.

'I thought so.' His mouth was tight now. His eyes swept over her figure in the revealing petticoat. 'At least anyone seeing us these last two nights could hardly be blamed for thinking that we know each other very well indeed. Don't forget that you spent last night in my arms. And from what I recall of the experience it was . . . tolerable for both of us.'

The uncomfortable undeniable truth of this brought a wave of scalding shame to Cindy's cheeks. 'And do you think that a bangle,' she used the word scornfully, 'however expensive is payment for that?'

There was a long ghastly silence when she realised that she had gone too far. Then at last he spoke, ice crackling in his voice.

'No. That thought had not entered my head. Curiously, I'm not in the habit of having to pay for such things. And I'm surprised that you would consider such a price insufficient. No,' and his voice took on a deceptively mild tone, 'I wanted to give you something and my mother told me that you had admired this. It isn't unusual for Arabs to give presents to their guests. And as you have been a guest in my mother's house . . . However,' he shrugged, lifted the box and slipped it into his pocket, 'I am sorry that I have offended you.' And before she could speak again, he had crossed the floor and the door had closed behind him.

How, oh how, thought Cindy in desperation, had she arrived at this situation? Why had she been so prickly when he had come along to her room? And why had she assumed at once that his intentions were dishonourable? After all, it was probably true what he said, he wasn't the kind to have to pay for women's favours. Even tonight it had been impossible not to notice how all the women at the party had kept darting curious little glances at him and when he had spoken to them, even the middle-aged ones had fluttered, flirted with him.

Desperately she threw off the rest of her clothes, pulled on her nightdress and lay shivering slightly, under the covers of the large bed. And to think, about half an hour ago, she had almost been inviting him to come along to her room to make love to her. And how amused he would have been when he realised her inexperience. No doubt all those other women he had referred to, knew exactly what they were doing. And how much more skilful they would be at satisfying a man like Adham.

And this thought, which surely

should have been comforting, had the most unexpected result. For she felt tears suddenly coursing down her cheeks, her body was wracked with violent sobs. Vaguely she hoped that perhaps he would hear, that he would be sorry and come in to tell her that it was all right, that they ought not to have quarrelled.

But of course he slept on the other side of the house and there wasn't the faintest chance that he would hear. Gradually the paroxysm eased. Cindy lay in the darkness, listening to the sound of her choked breathing. And at last she fell asleep.

11

Two days later, without seeing him again on her own, she flew out of Riyadh. As they soared above the desert, she told herself how glad she was that at last she was getting away from the fraught intense atmosphere of the house she had left. Not that anyone else had seemed to be aware of it.

The Sheikha had been her normal smiling gentle self when she returned early on the morning following the scene which had caused such anguish to her guest. And then when she had seen the sketches for the jewellery which Cindy had finished, she expressed her delight.

'But these are charming, Cindy, my dear.' Quickly she flicked over the pages. 'Exactly what I would have designed myself had I been able to do so.' She cast a swift discerning glance at the girl. 'You look a little tired? I hope you haven't been doing too much. Has Adham looked after you properly?'

'Yes. Very well.' She turned away in case her expression should be revealing. 'Have you seen him?'

'Yes. We met briefly in the courtyard but had no chance to do more than exchange a few words. He asked about his aunt.'

'Oh, I'm sorry. I should have, too. How is she?'

The Sheikha shrugged and sighed. 'She was a little brighter when I left. But she is still unhappy. I cannot think of a solution. But she has a good husband and I hope that in time she will learn to count her blessings.'

'I'm glad.' Cindy paused. 'Sheikha, please do you think I could ring the airport to enquire about bookings? I must get back to my work. I have been away so long.'

'Oh?' The Sheikha returned her attention to the sheaf of sketches. 'Well, they would be most ungrateful if they are less than delighted. I assure you that my order will be a very costly one and I'm sure it won't be the last. When my friends see what you have designed . . . Tell me,' suddenly she looked up at the girl, 'what gave you the idea of the designs?'

Cindy coloured, finding herself faced with the question she had been anxious to avoid. 'You see, Sheikha . . . Nevine is so different from anyone I have ever met . . . And you were right, it was only when I had seen her, met her that I had any idea at all.'

'And how would you describe the style.' The older woman waved a finger in a sweeping motion. 'So light and delicate, yet so . . . enclosed perhaps is the word.' A smile hovered about her mouth as she looked at Cindy.

'Oh.' The girl laughed. 'Will everyone notice that? I'm sorry. I thought of Nevine as a gorgeous bird but somehow caged, restrained, but by the most benign gaoler.' She amended tactfully.

'I shall forgive you.' There was a

snort of amusement from the older woman. 'Although I'm sorry you should see Nevine like that. She isn't, you know. Her parents died several years ago, I think I told you. And she could have chosen a freer life had she wished. But she prefers it as she is now. And what is more, the man she is to marry wishes it, too. You know, Cindy, many women who have been brought up like Nevine would be humiliated if a man should see their faces. Foolish to you and even to myself, I suppose. But Nevine feels that she has something very special to offer her husband.'

'Yes. I'm beginning to understand a little.'

'And don't worry. If Nevine sees what you have put into the designs, she will only be amused.'

Gaining confidence and longing for some escape from her own misery, Cindy began to explain enthusiastically some of the subtle points of what she had in mind. Using a fine pen, she showed the Sheikha how certain choices could be open, how the earrings, long pendants with tiny cage-like boxes at the ends could have tiny jewels set inside on short spindles.

'I see, the bird of paradise in a gilded cage,' the Sheikha said drily.

'Oh, no.' Then she saw the other woman's faint smile. 'Well, perhaps, if that's how you wish to describe it. From what you've said Nevine won't object to the reference.'

'Mmm.' Again the Sheikha consulted the papers. 'Well, I can think about that. Only I shan't settle things now. Tonight when Adham comes back I shall ask his advice and together we shall decide. I'm inclined to think of emeralds. With platinum I think there's little to compare, for pureness and clarity.'

'So you have decided on platinum? Well, either that or white gold would look stunning with emeralds. But if you preferred yellow gold, then perhaps a tiny cluster of rubies or sapphires . . . '

'Not rubies, I think. They are for

older women. But I shall decide tonight and I shall ring Mr Gascoigne in the morning.' How long do you think it will take, Cindy, to complete the order, I mean?'

'It will take some time. You see all this,' Cindy swiftly illustrated what she was saying, 'all this intricate filigree will be time-consuming. There aren't many craftsmen who could even attempt it and the work is so fine that those who can do it can concentrate for short periods only.'

'Yes, I can understand that. It's almost cobwebby in parts.'

'I should think at least three months for the complete set, if that's what you want, earrings, necklet and bracelet. You like the way I've incorporated the basic theme in the bracelet, do you, Sheikha? If you prefer to have the 'cages'' she smiled, 'dangling, then I can change them without too much trouble. Only I know that sometimes, especially with such fine work, they can catch on materials and such-like. And it would be awful if they should be damaged.'

'No, I'm sure that would be best.'

'On the other hand, I've just had an idea. I think I could arrange it so that they could be worn either way, clipped up into the bracelet, or hanging free. Yes, that's definitely possible.' She smiled at the Sheikha. 'I'll just go and make some quick sketches. I don't know why I didn't think of that before.' And she hurried off to the workroom, glad to be occupied with something that was so absorbing, something that would take her mind off — off other matters.

The rest of her time had passed so rapidly that she had had few opportunities to realise how miserable she was. To her surprise the house was filled with guests on her last evening, an arrangement she suspected Adham of suggesting to spare both of them the ordeal of a dinner á trois.

★　★　★

And now, she was simply grateful to be going home. She leaned back in her aircraft seat closing her eyes. Soon she would get over all this foolishness.

★   ★   ★

London seemed remarkably unchanged in the brief time she had been away. The lounge at the airport was its usual bustle of cosmopolitans and almost the first person she saw when she walked through the barrier was Fenton, Mr Gascoigne's chauffeur. She had expected him, of course, for her boss had sent that message via the Sheikha. And it was pleasant for her to be able to hand over her suitcases to him, to realise that soon she would be whisked home with no worries about waiting for a taxi.

'Had a good trip, did you miss?' He tucked the rug about her legs as he settled her in the back seat of the Rolls.

'Yes, thank you. I slept most of the way. But that,' she yawned, 'seems to

241

have made me sleepy.'

'Yes,' Fenton spoke over his shoulder as the car purred away from the kerb. 'Mr Gascoigne always says he feels tired when he's got back from his trips. I can't say I notice it much myself. Not when I go to Spain in the holidays.'

'That's true. I suppose it just depends on how you're feeling at the time.' And that she thought could explain a great deal under the circumstances.

'You'll be feeling the cold, too, I expect. We've had a raw few days.'

'Not in the car. But it was a bit shivery walking across from the plane. Has there been much rain?' She looked out on to the wet streets, saw the huddled pedestrians going about their business. Her eye recoiled from the dejection of the scene, rejected the rather squalid condition of the streets with the grubby litter adding to the air of neglect. That was one thing about Riyadh, she thought and then caught herself up. 'What did you say, Mr

Fenton?' She leaned forward in her seat as if anxious not to miss a word the chauffeur was saying about the British climate.

At least her room was the same, she thought, hurrying over to put a match to the gas fire. Home. With all its limitations and deficiencies, she was glad to be back there. And when she had pulled the curtains, shutting out the dismal rainy evening, she would settle down quite comfortably. She'd forget about that other place.

★　★　★

'I notice you're being very cagey about the Sheikh.' It was their first opportunity to speak since Cindy had started work again and after the initial excitement was over, Marjorie settled down to teasing her friend.

'I told you,' Cindy studied the menu with more attention than its limited choice deserved, 'I didn't see all that much of him. I'll have a cheese omelette.' She smiled at Marjorie, hoping that her friend would not see behind the façade. 'He was away for a lot of the time. He has business interests all over the Middle East. So his mother told me,' she added hastily.

'I still think,' Marjorie accepted the menu Cindy handed across but she didn't look at it, 'that if I had had your opportunity . . . Oh, well,' she grinned and shook her head, 'there's no use dreaming. The girl will be here in a minute to take our order.

'By the way,' Cindy took the opportunity to change the subject firmly when the girl had come and gone, 'what has happened to our dear Madeleine since I left? She was positively friendly when I arrived in the office yesterday.'

As she shook her head, Marjorie looked blank. 'I've no idea.' Then her face cleared a little. 'Unless . . . ' She hesitated.

'Unless what?' Cindy took up her knife and fork, looking at the omelette which had been put in front of her. 'Unless what?' She raised her head in surprise at Marjorie's reticence.

'Perhaps I shouldn't say,' began Marjorie unexpectedly.

Cindy snorted. 'That would be unlike you!'

'Yes, it would,' agreed Marjorie equably. 'It's nothing really. But I did notice — I don't see her much you know — But one day I saw her arriving. She drives that little white Mini, the one — '

'I know, I know,' said Cindy impatiently. 'I've seen her arrive in it.'

'Well, I just thought, that she had been buying new clothes. She looked much more with it than she usually does. You know she always wears such dreary outfits . . . '

'Yes, that's true,' said Cindy thoughtfully. 'To me they've always seemed more suitable to her grandmother than herself. She can't be so very old. Thirty-one, thirty-two.'

'About that. And another thing . . . '

Marjorie chased the last little piece of omelette round her plate, 'the other night I saw her driving away from that parking spot at the back. She pretended she hadn't seen me, not that that's unusual, but she had a man in the car beside her. And, now that I think of it, it could just have been the boss.' She looked across the table, her face a comical study in dismay. 'I wonder Cindy . . . Do you think it's possible that they're having an affair?'

'I should think it's highly unlikely.'

'Well' Marjorie, having hit on a likely explanation, was reluctant to relinquish it. 'He has that reputation, you know.'

'But he's got a wife and family, hasn't he? I remember not so long ago, Madeleine came into his office with a message that he should remember the fish.' Suddenly she giggled. 'Imagine anyone having the nerve to send him those instructions.'

'I've heard that his wife keeps him under her thumb. At least she tries to. But of course, he has this little weakness . . . ' She paused. 'But I thought that he was a friend of your family, love? You should know more about him than I do.'

'Oh, I know nothing about him personally. I hadn't even met him before I came for the interview. Only, my father's family had known his for years. I think our grandparents were cousins or something.'

'Well, we'll just have to keep our eyes open. It'll be easier for you.' There was mischief in the dark expressive face. 'It would be too funny if we found out that old Gaskers and our dear Miss Grange were having a torrid affair. It might be the making of her.'

'Oh, Marjorie, it wouldn't be all that easy for her.' Cindy felt a swift burst of sympathy for the secretary. 'It would be bound to finish some time. And what would she be like then? She's so intense . . . Anyway . . . ' She took a firm grip of herself. 'This is all the wildest speculation. Let's forget about the emotional problems of our betters.

What about you and Rick? Is there any chance of his move to London?'

But later, when she was busy at her desk, Cindy reflected on what Marjorie had told her. There was no doubt about it, something had happened to work a change in Madeleine Grange. Not only had she thawed considerably towards Cindy, her whole attitude in life seemed to have undergone a transformation. The old top quality dress and jacket outfits which were so right, so stuffy had gone. These days she was wearing pretty skirt and bolero sets with feminine blouses. And today, she had on a fitting dress in a particularly attractive shade of green. It was all quite intriguing although, she assured herself again, there was no evidence that it had anything to do with Mr Gascoigne.

So life at Daubeny and Gascoigne's went on as usual and soon it seemed to Cindy that she might never have been away. That party in the desert began to assume an air of fantasy, and occasionally Cindy wondered if she had dreamed the whole thing. Only the constant ache in her chest told her otherwise, and the recollection of those times when she had lain in his arms brought the pain surging back with sharp intensity.

December came in with cold flurries of snow that made Cindy think longingly of warmer climes. Sternly she forced her mind away from such dangerous paths and tried to think of the suggestion that her mother had made in a recent letter.

'*Charles and I are so anxious to have you come out on a visit, Cindy. It seems such ages since we saw you and I must confess I'm longing to see my only child. Don't laugh, even the least maternal sometimes has natural inclinations.*' (Cindy smiled when she read that. How often she had teased her mother for her abnormal willingness to allow her daughter to go her own way) '*We thought Christmas might be an opportune moment and you haven't said that you've made any arrangements for the holiday. Do you think Mr Gascoigne could bear to part with you for a few weeks?'*

Then the letter had gone on to tell Cindy what her mother had been doing to fill in her time, to tempt her with all kinds of extravagant plans for the Christmas holiday. But there was a P.S. which forced Cindy to realise that perhaps she herself wasn't quite so good at hiding her feelings as she had thought.

'P.S. You've sounded a bit down in your letters, darling. Since you got back from Riyadh, that is. I hope you haven't picked up some kind of bug!'

Cindy, when she had read it, let the letter drop from her fingers to the floor. For a long time she sat, staring into the hissing candles of the gas fire, the present completely forgotten as she went back to the last time she had seen him.

They had driven in to Riyadh airport,

a quiet, rather intense trio. Even Cindy, immersed as she was in her own pain had been conscious of that. Adham, tight-lipped at the wheel of the car had said little and the Sheikha who had tried to speak brightly had found her remarks answered in monosyllables. Once or twice she had turned to look at Cindy in the rear seat, had smiled apologetically as if asking that her son's bad manners might be excused. And her glance had surely taken in the fact that their guest, too, was strained and silent.

What deduction she made from such an obvious coincidence Cindy could scarcely guess. There was no doubt that the Sheikha would have heard about the foolish episode when she had rushed off into the desert. And she would know that they had returned together in the early hours of the morning. There was only one conclusion that could be drawn from that.

It occurred to Cindy, not for the first time, that perhaps the Sheikha had had such an idea in her mind from the first. She had sensed that her son had been attracted to the girl in the shop and had done her best to see that they were thrown together. It was all so convenient and if that had been her plan it had all worked perfectly. Only, Cindy couldn't quite believe that the Sheikha would be as coldly devious or cruel. It would take a particularly unprincipled woman to procure, and Cindy shivered as she thought of that word, a young woman for her son.

But almost as soon as she thought of it, Cindy dismissed the notion from her mind. The Sheikha was too kind to behave like that. And there was no doubt at all that when Cindy left, there had been tears in the older woman's eyes, she had shaken her head, laughing a little as if at her own foolishness.

'I shall see you when next I come to London, Cindy. I shall be calling to collect the jewellery when it is ready. In the meantime, my dear,' she had taken a package from her handbag to hand to the girl, 'this is from me. My son has told me that I ought not to embarrass you by offering anything of value, so this is something small.' She had pressed her cheek to Cindy's for a moment before turning away, her handkerchief to her face.

Then Cindy had felt the torture of her hand being held in Adham's. This time there had been no flashing lights, no crashing cymbals, merely the dumb anguish of knowing that this was the last time she would see him. She felt her lips twist in the formality of a smile, sought in vain some response from him. But there was no friendliness in the sea-green look.

'Goodbye, Cindy.' He was totally unmoved by the occasion. 'Have a safe journey.' The banal words he would have used to any departing business-man.

And that had been the last she saw of them. She had turned swiftly, the sound of her tapping heels on the tiled floor marking an end, just like the row of asterisks at the foot of a printed page. Then she was out of the huge air-conditioned building and into the blazing heat of that impossible land.

Cindy leaned forward to turn down the heat from the fire. Sitting as close as she now was, she was getting the full force of it on her face.

From the carpet where it had fallen she picked up the airmail letter and the final words sprang at her from the page.

'*I hope you haven't picked up some kind of bug.*'

A bitter little smile twisted her mouth. Some kind of bug. If she could only take a detached view she was sure she would find it funny. For in a way she had picked up a bug. Self-pityingly she wished it had been a malaria mosquito, or perhaps a mild dose of plague. At least a visit from a doctor and a few injections might be likely to cure her. But for the sickness that was afflicting her, she was certain there was no remedy in the whole world.

12

Two days later, Cindy had made up her mind. Suddenly she couldn't bear the thought of being alone in her flat over Christmas. Marjorie was going home and although she had assured Cindy that she would be welcome to go north with her, Cindy knew that Rick was spending the holiday with his future in-laws, too, and she had no inclination to be an unwelcome third on their outings.

In an effort to dispel such a notion, Marjorie had suggested, rather tentatively for her, that Jamie didn't live too far away and that if Cindy crooked her little finger . . .

'No.' The refusal had been an instant reflex action which was tempered by a reluctant smile. 'No. Thank you, love. You know that weekend after I came back . . . It wasn't really a success.' She remembered with distaste Jamie's attempts at passionate love-making.

'Yes, you told me that at the time. Although I can't see what the problem is. I think he's quite an attractive man. And if you're going to be my bridesmaid, and he's to be best man . . . '

'I didn't know there was any rule about that. That they had to be in love with each other as well as the bride and bridegroom!'

'Oh, you!' Marjorie pushed her friend laughingly. 'You know what I mean.'

'Yes. And the point is, love, that I think Jamie and I will be on much better terms at your wedding if he and I don't see too much of each other before then. You have decided on the sixteenth of February?' Firmly she turned the conversation away from her relationship with the best man and towards a subject which she knew would keep Marjorie interested indefinitely.

That conversation pushed Cindy into her decision and the following day, feeling rather nervous about the request she was going to make, she asked to see Mr Gascoigne. When she was shown into his office, she thought she detected a trace of concern, followed by an expression of relief when she explained what she wanted.

'So,' he summed up when she had finished, 'what you want is an extension of the Christmas break; you want to take some of your annual holiday then to enable you to spend Christmas with your mother in America?'

'Yes. If it's convenient to you.'

'Well . . . I think that can be arranged.' He smiled at her across the top of his large desk. 'I think in view of the important business you have recently brought to the firm, we should be very ungrateful if we refused you. So, just let me know when you are going and when we may expect you back and I'm sure it will be all right.' He paused to pick up a piece of paper from the blotting pad in front of him. 'I'm glad you came in this morning,

Cindy. It saves me the trouble of sending for you. Just an hour ago I had some enquiries about designs from someone in Wiltshire.' He consulted the paper he held in his hand. 'Yes, a Mr O'Neill from a place called Lowyn Hall, near Bardford.' He looked up at her with a smile. 'He has heard of our Nefertiti collection from a friend and is anxious to see the designs. I suggest, and it's only a suggestion, my dear, that perhaps you would like to take them down so that you can explain them to him yourself. You seem to have a way with you when it comes to getting orders.'

'When do you want me to go, Mr Gascoigne? I have these designs to complete for those bridesmaids gifts, the ones ordered by Lord Pelham.'

'Let me see now. What was it he wanted, six pendants and bracelets for four children is that right?'

'Yes, but the problem was that he wanted the family crest illustrated in the designs. And it's not too easy,' a faint smile crossed her face, 'to incorporate a charging boar in something suitable for young girls and children.'

'I can see the difficulty.' Mr Gascoigne twinkled at her. 'But I'm sure you'll cope well enough. How much longer will you require to prepare, my dear — two, three days perhaps?'

'I think that ought to be long enough. Most of the planning has been done. Now it's mainly a case of preparing some finished designs so that they can choose. That could be completed by Thursday.'

'Then I shall ring Mr O'Neill and tell him you'll be down on Friday. It would be best not to keep him waiting longer than necessary. That's why so many firms lose customers. Oh, and by the way, Cindy, you can have Fenton to take you there and bring you home again. I don't know if you'll be able to travel back on Friday. But if you have to stay somewhere overnight, it won't matter. I find,' and suddenly he was very busy making notes on a piece of paper, 'I find that I shall have to stay in town overnight on Friday so I shan't require the car.'

As she closed the door of the office, Cindy found none of the disapproval that had characterised her previous dealings with the secretary. Today, Madeleine Grange positively beamed at Cindy as she walked across the outer office. Then she herself got up with alacrity and swept purposefully across to the door of the inner sanctum.

Cindy smiled to herself as she returned to her own desk. In her own mind, what had before been more conjecture was now more or less confirmed. It was so obvious that Madeleine, who had been crabbed and miserable with a grudge against her own sex, was now happy and fulfilled. And was it too much to suppose that Mr Gascoigne, with his reputation for philandering might have something to do with the transformation? Anyway, it was none of her business but it certainly made working conditions much easier. And quite apart from other considerations, it was nice to see someone so happy. If only her own unhappiness could be so quickly solved.

Aware of the familiar twist of pain, Cindy grabbed her pen. There was no time for self-indulgence with so much work to cope with. Today she would finalise her drafts, tomorrow . . . then Thursday. Yes, if she got on with the job, she could just manage to be free for the journey to Wiltshire on Friday. It would be something to look forward to. That and her trip to the States at Christmas. She must ring down and tell Marjorie that she wouldn't be able to go with her for lunch today, she would have to go to the travel agent instead.

★   ★   ★

How beautiful the countryside looked after a night of heavy frost and with the sun shining from a sky of clear pale blue. They skimmed quietly along the

261

motorway, thankful to have left the congested streets of the city behind, appreciating with all the enthusiasm of the Londoner the beauty of the uncrowded countryside.

Trees were thicky frosted, the tracery of glittering faceted white delighting Cindy so that she found her hand itching for a pen and pad. But she hadn't thought to bring her tools into the car with her, instead they were languishing in the boot along with her folio of drawings and the overnight bag she had brought with her in case they decided to stay the night.

They had been promised that lunch would be available for them when they reached their destination but Cindy was pleased when Fenton suggested they should stop for a cup of coffee. She hadn't eaten much at breakfast and now felt in need of some refreshment. Besides it would give her the opportunity to tidy up before they reached Lowyn Hall.

'You're looking very bonny this

morning, Miss Charles.' Mr Fenton's friendly eyes smiled at her.

'Thank you, Mr Fenton. I just bought this last week.' Cindy smoothed down the warm bouclé wool coat thinking that if it hadn't been for the generous bonus she had got from the firm she would never have been able to afford it. 'It's really for my holiday in the States. Did you know I was going out to spend Christmas with my mother?'

'Aye, I did hear that. Some people have all the luck! Last month Riyadh, this New York. There'll be no holding you soon.'

'Oh, I don't think so. When this trip's over I'll have to stay put. It's too expensive to do anything else.'

'That's true. My wife and I were supposed to be going to Majorca this year but the prices in the packages keep going up every time.' He pushed back his chair. 'Have you finished then, Miss?'

'Yes. If you can just wait while I go

and wash my hands.'

In the ladies' room Cindy surveyed herself critically in the long mirror. She was pleased with her coat with its long slender lines and small fur collar which matched the cossack style hat she had bought last year. She pulled on the smooth black gloves, checked that her boots were polished and shiny before turning to the door.

As they travelled through the small town of Barford, Cindy was aware of a mounting excitement which she couldn't have explained. After all, it wasn't the first time she'd had to take designs direct to a customer. Even before her trip to Saudi Arabia she had made two such visits. She could only imagine that her experiences in Riyadh had changed her attitude to this kind of job. Mentally she shook herself. How long was she going to continue this idiotic looking back?'

Fenton seemed to know the area for he found his way through the network of minor roads with no apparent difficulty and just before one o'clock they turned into a concealed gateway and drove up a long tree lined drive. They approached the house from the rear, following the gravel drive round to the front where the Rolls drew to a perfect gentle stop.

The house was smaller than Cindy had anticipated from the length of the drive and the quality of the surrounding parkland. There were several large buildings at the rear of the house, beautifully kept and seeming to indicate that the owner had a considerable interest in horses. On one side of the drive they had passed a field with several jumps set out which confirmed the impression she had gained.

Realising that Fenton was holding open the door of the car for her, Cindy climbed out, standing on the gravel and looking around.

'This is your brief case, Miss. I'll take the car round to the back. You can let me know when you're ready to leave.'

'Yes. Thank you, Mr Fenton.' Cindy

265

hitched her black handbag on to her shoulder and took the brief case from him. 'Then I'll see you later.'

When the car had circled the large apron outside the house, Cindy turned towards the short flight of steps that ran up to the front door. But on the top step, before she raised her hand to pull the heavy brass ring that would bring someone to let her in, she turned to savour again the tranquillity of the scene in front of her. She could imagine the colours that would riot about the paving in the spring. Between the old flagstones and in the huge mellow urns she could recognise the foliage of hellebores, primula and bergenia. On the lower terrace, separated from the upper by a few shallow steps and a low wall, she could see a border of camellia and further away a small round lily pond, thickly frosted and with the water nymph in the centre raising her arms in a gesture of supplication. Probably praying for summer, thought Cindy with a wry smile as she turned at last to pull the bell.

'Miss Charles?' The housekeeper was a tall, capable looking woman who surveyed Cindy with a somewhat curious glance. 'Come in. Mr O'Neill is expecting you. If you would like to bring your coat in here.' She led the way into a comfortable cloakroom and helped her off with her coat. 'I'll leave you to wash your hands, miss, and then I'll show you into the morning room. And I'll have Mr O'Neill called. He told me to let him know as soon as you arrived.'

The sharp air had brought the colour to Cindy's cheeks but a touch of powder from her compact put that right. When she had run a comb through her hair, she went out into the hall where she found the housekeeper hovering.

'I'll take you through the fire, Miss Charles.' She smiled as her glance moved approvingly over the girl. 'It's a cold day and I'm sure you'll be pleased to see a nice blaze.'

The log fire was a gorgeous heart-lifting sight and Cindy, with an explanation of pleasure, sank down on to one of the chintz covered easy chairs, holding out her hands to the warmth.

'What a beautiful room!' She smiled up at the older woman.

'Yes, I think that every day.' She bent down to sweep up an imaginary speck of ash from the marble hearth. 'Would you like a glass of sherry now, Miss Charles, or would you prefer to wait till Mr O'Neill comes? He won't be more than a few minutes,' she added.

'Oh, I'll wait.'

'Then lunch will be about two. I've put it back a little as Mr O'Neill said you would want to talk for a bit first. And I'll see that Mr Fenton has his meal right away.'

When the door had closed behind the housekeeper, Cindy pulled her brief-case close to the side of the chair; it looked as if some of the work would be done before lunch. So probably there would be no trouble reaching home tonight. And the weekend yawned emptily ahead of her.

She sat back in the chair, looking about her with interest. On either side of the fireplace were tall arched windows looking out on to the drive that swept round the side of the house. On the adjoining wall with views over the terrace and lily pond were glass doors which she imagined would be thrown wide open in the summer. The room was really very attractive, the covers on the chairs picking up the soft rose of the carpet and velvet curtains and several pieces of old furniture polished to a rare patina. In one corner stood a mahogany cupboard, with some ornately decorated pieces of china displayed. Everything about the room was so beautifully English, Cindy thought. She rose from her seat and went over to study the small picture which hung on the plain white wall between the glass doors.

It was, as seemed appropriate, an oil

painting of two bays and a dog beside a lake in a wooded landscape. Cindy was particularly interested by the technique used on the sky, with a golden sun threatening to appear from behind some heavy clouds. In the bottom right she thought she could detect the name Leakey but it was difficult to make out properly. In any case, it seemed to be the sort of picture that would appeal to a man with Mr O'Neill's interests, horses, dogs and pleasant English countryside.

But he wasn't too horsey, Cindy decided, for about the room were little touches that could come only from a man of taste. She noticed on one of the small tables a pile of magazines which would interest antique collectors and behind one of the glass cupboards was a collection of novels and literary reference books which gave the impression of being more than adjuncts to impress visitors.

In fact, Cindy wandered about the room restlessly and somewhat impatiently, she was becoming anxious to meet Mr O'Neill who was a rather mysterious figure as far as Daubeny and Gascoigne were concerned. None of the other members of the staff had heard of him and even the boss had seemed reluctant to discuss him or to say what exactly his original enquiries had been.

When she had spoken of it with Marjorie, Cindy had found that the other girl was quite astonished at such a long journey to woo a customer who was so totally unknown to the firm.

'I think old Gaskers is beginning to go a bit funny. Perhaps it's this affair with Madeleine that's causing premature aging. Maybe he can't keep up with both a wife and a mistress.'

'Marjorie! We don't know that she is. Maybe they just enjoy going to the theatre together or — '

'Yes, I know. Or looking at his etchings. Well, if you believe that. But about your trip to Wiltshire . . . I've never heard of him giving one of his employees the Rolls for the weekend. You'd better watch or Miss Grange will be getting jealous again. Or maybe,' and she had gone off at another tangent, 'maybe he's trying to throw you and John Fenton together. I wonder if he's discovered that his chauffeur has been nursing a hopeless passion for you and he would like everyone to be as happy as he is himself with his Indian summer romance.'

'I shouldn't think that's likely.' Cindy had grown used to Marjorie's wildly romantic nonsense and treated it with casual amusement. 'At least, not to the extent of lending his Rolls to further the course of true love. And I thought that you told me that Mr Fenton has a very nice wife whom he's very fond of.'

'Yes, that's true. Anyway, I've rather gone off that idea. He's too old for you. And there's something funny about it all . . .'

Remembering, Cindy smiled to herself and put out a hand for one of the magazines. Marjorie seemed to exist in one long daydream filled with all kinds of exciting, wholly unlikely adventures in which her friends featured. They never included herself, or at least if they did, her role was usually that of a confidante and advisor. It was strange that such a dreamer should be such a very competent salesgirl. And it was also surprising that she should be about to marry such a very ordinary boy. Rick was a pleasant enough young man but to Cindy's eye there seemed little about him to intrigue someone as romantic as Marjorie. And yet, when they were together, there seemed very little doubt that they were very deeply in love. A knife unexpectedly twisted in her chest and feverishly she leafed through the pages, trying to concentrate on what she was reading.

So successful was she that she didn't hear the almost soundless opening of the door. But its closing was more firm and definite, making her turn round, a smile and an expression of apology on her lips. But the words were never uttered. The smile faded to be replaced by a grimace of disbelief and pain.

Gone were the thobe and headcloth, all the appurtenances of the desert and in their place the everyday clothes of the English countryman. But the face was as dear, as unmistakable as ever.

13

It might have been a moment or an eternity that they stood looking at each other but the burst of anguish in her breast seemed endless. So absorbed was she in her own torment that she was blind to the reflection of something approaching her own feelings portrayed so clearly on his features. Her instinct was to run from him, away from these elegant persuasive surroundings, down the impressive tree-lined drive in search of some dark corner where she could throw herself down and weep. And weep until there was some relief from this crippling misery. But while he looked at her she could not move, could not escape the intensity of her own emotions nor the words which he was about to speak.

'Cindy.' Her name sounded like a caress on his lips, she clenched her hands to control the trembling while she searched the green eyes for some indication of what was happening. 'Cindy.' It was a sigh now, soft with yearning, so lovingly spoken that she felt the almost irresistible prick of tears behind her eyes. Tears which he must not be allowed to see. He put out his hands to take hers but resolutely she thrust them into the pockets of her blue dress.

'What are you doing here?' Her voice was harsher than she had intended. Harsher than was necessary but its coldness helped her to retain control.

'This is my home.' He spoke quietly, his eyes never seeming to leave her face.

His home. Of course. It was well known that rich foreigners were buying up property all over the country. The pain that she was suffering made her bitter and sarcastic. 'Your ancestral home, I suppose.' Then without giving him the opportunity to reply, 'I was asked to come here to speak to a Mr O'Neill. I suppose he does exist?' Just

276

in time she caught her lower lip between her teeth stifling the sob that threatened to escape.

'Yes.' He spoke with a mildness that suggested her pointed rudeness had been lost on him. 'Yes. He exists.' He turned and walked to the side table where some glasses and a decanter stood on a silver tray. 'May I offer you sherry?'

'Thank you.' In agitation she turned back to the fire, watching him in the mirror, seeing him turn towards her with two glasses. 'I see that alcohol is allowed here.' The sarcastic note was back in her voice but the hand that was raising the glass to her lips scarcely trembled.

'I know of no laws against it.' He seemed determined not to lose patience and that in itself was an annoyance, more especially when she was trying so hard to provoke him. He raised his glass in a salute which she decided was mocking. 'To you, Cindy.' His face was rather grave.

She looked at him without replying, wishing, wishing that she could escape from the misery of love. If she could have discovered that it was simply the romance and enchantment of the desert, how happy she would have been. Only one finger, tapping nervously against her side betrayed her agitation and when at last she spoke her voice was amazingly calm.

'Mr O'Neill, the man whom I have come to see. When shall I be able to speak to him?'

'Now.' His eyes, guarded and mysterious, held hers as she whirled round from the fire. Her control had snapped, her breast heaved as she watched his mouth, heard him say words that she could not understand although she had known from the moment he had stepped into the room. 'I am O'Neill.'

Before she realised what he was about he had relieved her of her glass and had caught hold of both of her hands. Instantly that familiar trickle of longing which she had been fighting to quench, burst out of control and enveloped her like a raging fire. She made a last futile effort to drag her hands from his but he was irresistible. A sob of weakness, frustrated yearnings, even a trace of anger at the treacherous weakness of her own body broke from her lips.

'Cindy.' His soft tenderness was infinitely beguiling. 'Cindy.' She was pulled closer so that she could see, a mere inch from her eyes, the brown and green check of his jacket. He was so English that he might indeed have been who he claimed to be. He might have been telling the truth . . . only she knew differently.

There was no resistance as his hand came beneath her chin to turn her face up to his. The silky touch of beard took her back at once to that other night, finally proving it had not been simply the magic of the desert. For the same explosion of fire ran through her veins when his lips claimed hers and she had no will, no inclination but to respond meltingly.

'My darling.' Gently he traced the curve of her cheek. 'I can't tell you how I've longed for this.'

'But why . . . ' Her mind too clouded with delicious trembling emotions to begin to reason, Cindy leaned against him, her head on his chest. ' . . . Why didn't you just ask me to come. Instead of concocting such an involved plan?'

'Shh.' She felt two fingers being laid against her mouth before she was pulled down on to the settee alongside the fire. 'Don't say any more now.' And for a long trembling time neither of them spoke. At last he held her away from him, pressing her against the soft cushions. 'Do you trust me, Cindy?' He smoothed the hair back from her face.

'Yes.' It was the simple truth and with that acknowledgement a wave of relief swept through her. Of course she trusted him. What he asked of her, she would give. And willingly for she would be powerless to refuse him. 'Yes, I trust you.' And now longing to be total in her giving she linked her hands round his neck and pulled his face towards hers. 'Of course I do.'

He smiled and now there was a flash of amusement in the mysteriously green eyes. 'So you are prepared to trust a man whom you believe is masquerading under a false name?'

'Yes.' She moved her head slightly against the cushion. 'I suppose I'm crazy. But I do.'

'I love you. You know that.' His fingers moved tantalisingly against the nape of her neck.

Her lips curved in a smile of pure joy. 'And I love you quite madly.'

'And you will marry me? Soon?' The words were so soft that she wondered if she had heard properly. Her eyes shot open, gazing at him in surprise. Astonishment and consternation were both apparent when she spoke.

'Marry you?'

'What else had you in mind?' Although he looked perfectly serious she had a delicious sense of being teased.

'Nothing else. You see,' She paused while she ran her fingers down his face, stopping only when he caught them in his hands and held them to his lips. 'I really never thought that I should see you again. And then, when you came into the room . . . I still can't believe it, can't understand.'

'Then before I try to explain, answer my question. Lucinda, will you do me the honour of becoming my wife?'

'Oh, Adham . . . ' Her voice quavered just a little. 'Don't tease.'

'I was never more serious about anything. But I confess I feel just a bit 'high' at the moment. After so much misunderstanding.'

'Then if you mean it,' she pulled his head close to hers in an embrace that contained just a hint of desperation, 'yes, I shall marry you, Sheikh Adham. Or Mr O'Neill. Whoever you are.'

The sound of a gong, distant but distinct echoed through the house penetrating even into the blissful state of euphoria of the morning-room.

Adham sat up with a groan of reluctance, pushing back the lock of dark hair that had fallen over his forehead.

'I suppose we must. Or shall we stay here and embarrass Mrs Robinson when she comes along to remind us? Only to find us in a compromising situation on the sofa.'

'Perhaps . . . ' She kissed his mouth lingeringly, 'perhaps we ought to go.'

In the dining room they sat close together where it was possible for them to touch hands between courses. At last when they had eaten their way through grilled trout, casserole of pheasant and a tangy lemon dessert, they were left alone in the morning-room with a pot of coffee and no fear of further interruption.

'Can you forgive me, Cindy?'

'Of course I can. But I still can't understand. And I don't know why I have to forgive . . . '

'For all this.' He waved a hand in the direction of the window. 'For not telling you the truth about myself.'

'It wasn't any of my business. Not then. And it isn't unusual for Arabs to have homes in England as well as in their country.'

'But that is where I have deceived you most of all my sweet. You see,' he looked down at his cup as he stirred sugar into it, 'I'm not really an Arab.'

Cindy stared, unable to take in what he was trying to tell her. 'But your mother. The Sheikha.'

'I should have said I'm only half-Arab. My father was English. He met my mother during the war and they married against the wishes of both families.'

'But Adham . . . '

His mouth twisted into a slight smile. 'Yes, that is my name. But spelled in the English way. It was a name that satisfied both sides, so you see, my dear, you'll be Mrs Adam O'Neill.'

'Mrs Adam O'Neill.' She savoured the name for a moment before turning to him with some of the questions bubbling from her lips. 'But your father. And this house. And the Sheikha. It's all so complicated, Adam.'

'Yes, it is. And you'll have to be patient while I explain. But before we go any further, darling, do you think you could tell your driver to go back to London and you can stay the weekend.'

Although the suggestion was almost irresistible she made a mild objection. 'But what will he think? And Mrs Robinson?' But even as she spoke her eyes were telling him that of course she would stay the weekend. Mr Fenton came in so she was able to explain about the change of plan and it seemed to Cindy that he showed very little surprise but merely told her that he would put off her case and that he would see her back in town.

After that, while Adam was giving instructions to the housekeeper about the 'rose bedroom', Cindy took the opportunity of calling Mr Gascoigne. He listened quietly while she told him what she had decided, insisting that she would be able to get back to London on her own.

'That's fine, Cindy. And I'm so glad that everything has worked out well for you.' The girl stared at the receiver before she replaced it on its cradle. She was beginning to realise that she had been the victim of a deliberate plot. And that her employer was much less uncomplicated than anyone meeting him casually would have believed. First his affair with Madeleine Grange about which Cindy no longer had any doubt, and now these complex machinations to bring her to Lowyn Hall. The sound of the door opening interrupted her musings, bringing her round to face him with a smile.

'Fixed it up with your boss?' His mouth whispered against her cheek.

'Yes. You and he have been plotting to — ' The words were lost as his lips sought hers and the wild tempest of emotion pulled at her again.

'And are you sorry?' At last he held

her from him. 'That I persuaded your boss to let me have you?'

'It's nothing to do with Mr Gascoigne,' she said primly. 'He has enough to do with his own affairs.'

'Oh, I see. Then let's forget about him. Frankly all I want to think about is us. When shall we arrange the wedding? Shall I get a special licence so that we can be married at Christmas?'

'Oh, I couldn't possibly be ready in time. Besides,' She remembered something that had been swept from her mind. 'I'm going to New York at Christmas to stay with my mother and Charles.'

'Then I shall come with you. They won't mind that, will they?'

'No. I imagine they'll be thrilled. A real live Sheikh,' she teased.

He grimaced slightly. 'Well, I ought to complete the story. You asked about my father. He died when I was six. He had been badly wounded in the war and never really recovered.'

'Adam, I'm sorry. If you don't want

to go into all this now . . . '

'No. You must hear it. I want to tell you everything there is to tell about me. Besides I want the whole deception to be cleared up. As I told you, my parents married without the approval of their families but it was much more difficult for my mother's parents to accept. The O'Neill grandparents came round fairly quickly but for several years the Al Adhams tried to persuade my mother to renounce her marriage and go back to the old ways. In those days it was very unusual for an Arab woman to marry a European. Even today, you know how different their ways are.'

A vision of Nevine slipped into Cindy's mind and she shivered, thinking what the Sheikha must have had to endure.

'After I was born they relented a little,' Adam continued, 'and tried to make it a condition of their acceptance that I was brought up as an Arab. Of course, my father refused but he did agree that I should spend as much time in Riyadh as my mother wished until I had to go to school. After that only the holidays could be spent in Arabia. So I grew up equally at home in both cultures, although perhaps always something of an outsider in the Arab one, not wholly acceptable. Then when my father died, the pressure increased for my mother and me to live permanently in Riyadh. It must have been difficult to resist. And yet she did and I shall never be able to repay her for that. But from then my mother spent more time with her parents coming here during the school holidays so that we could both spend a few weeks with my father's parents. And you asked,' he grinned suddenly, teasingly at her, 'if this was my ancestral home and the answer is yes. The O'Neills bought this land when they came from Ireland in the mid-eighteenth century and the house was built about eighteen-ten. So, such as it is, it's the ancestral home of the O'Neills.'

'The poor Sheikha. How she must have suffered! So much being pulled in different directions.'

'Yes. And I was determined that should happen to no one I fell in love with. So much so that when we met I was about to give up all the English side of my life, and try to fit in completely with the Arab. But meeting you made me realise how impossible that was, my sweet. Struggle as I might to ignore what I was feeling for you. Then in the end I knew that it was useless. You were as much part of me as my right arm. But I was determined that you would not have to endure the pressures my mother suffered.'

'But she has done it. Other women have done it. And I imagine that many of them have thought it worth while. I would have done it. For you.' Tenderly she kissed him. 'You told me yourself that Nazir and Betty were perfectly happy. And we should not, at least,' she amended surveying him teasingly through a fringe of dark lashes, 'I hope we should not have the added difficulties of another wife and family.'

'No.' He laughed. 'That I can promise, my sweet. I've always suspected you were around somewhere, I've just been waiting for you to turn up. No, that is one difficulty we won't have. But, if we accepted the Arab way of life there would be others in abundance.'

'But I should hate to come between you and your mother. She must have been so happy when she thought you had decided to live in Arabia.'

'She will understand. No one better. And I really think that after so many years in England she almost considers herself English. Perhaps when she has some grandchildren she will decide to come here to live. Not here at Lowyn. But close by.'

'Mmm.' All his talk of children had for the moment robbed Cindy of speech but it was very temporary. 'Yes, that would be the ideal situation. I hope she approves of me. Perhaps she will be sorry that you aren't going to marry someone she knows better.'

'I think I can reassure you. In fact I think she has known from the first just how I felt about you. Even before I dared admit it to myself. Remember that bracelet you were too proud to accept? You don't think it's usual to give such gifts, do you? And how can she possibly disapprove when she did the same thing herself? And in much less enlightened times than now. Oh, and when we go upstairs remind me to give you that bracelet. I was so angry with it that I threw it into the back of the drawer, determined to forget you. Did you really think,' he smoothed back the hair from her face, 'that I was trying to pay you for something?'

'No.' Remembering her dramatic rejection of the bracelet she giggled suddenly. 'And I'm sorry I was rude to you.'

'Hmm.' He held her away, looking down with an appraising expression. 'You don't look sorry, I must say. And you ought to be. You gave me the worst moments of my life, I suppose you realise that? Running off into a sandstorm! I ought to have thought of some suitable punishment. But all I could think of was that I had found you.'

'Oh?' Her voice was muffled against his jacket. 'I must say, if you felt relief you hid it very well.'

'But seriously, Cindy, have you any idea just how close to death you came?' His face had grown serious. 'Too many people have simply disappeared, a moment's carelessness and there are no second chances with the desert. Promise me that you will never take such risks again.'

When she had promised and he had shown again how relieved he was at her narrow escape, they sat talking while the early winter dusk fell and they were at last disturbed by the rattle of crockery as Mrs Robinson wheeled the tea trolley along the corridor. And then later while she poured cups of tea to drink with the hot buttered scones, he lay back in his armchair watching her, a picture of total content, legs stretched out to the crackling log fire.

'In one thing my sweet, I must tell you, the Arab part of me is dominant. And you must accept that.'

'Yes?' Although she smiled, one part of her felt a flicker of apprehension. He sounded so serious and she couldn't bear it if anything should come between them now.

'To the Arab, his women are more precious than anything in the world, more protected, more cared for. That, strange as it may seem, is why Nevine is as she is.'

'Yes, I know.' And indeed now she could accept what had been unacceptable. Some Arabs protected their women to the extent that they would allow no one to look on their faces. And it was what they wanted even in the rapidly changing world. So why should anyone else object? She nodded. 'I do understand now. And I accept your conditions,' she ended teasingly.

'Then,' with one easy movement he

came to stand in front of her, pulling her gently to her feet. 'So long as that is firmly understood. From this moment you are the most important being in my world. Even more than you were before. And I will go even further than most Arabs . . . ' His mouth caressed her hair. ' . . . Even more precious to me than a hundred camels, thou art.'

We do hope that you have enjoyed reading this large print book.

Did you know that all of our titles are available for purchase?

We publish a wide range of high quality large print books including:
Romances, Mysteries, Classics
General Fiction
Non Fiction and Westerns

Special interest titles available in large print are:
The Little Oxford Dictionary
Music Book, Song Book
Hymn Book, Service Book

Also available from us courtesy of Oxford University Press:
Young Readers' Dictionary
(large print edition)
Young Readers' Thesaurus
(large print edition)

For further information or a free brochure, please contact us at:
Ulverscroft Large Print Books Ltd.,
The Green, Bradgate Road, Anstey,
Leicester, LE7 7FU, England.
Tel: (00 44) **0116 236 4325**
Fax: (00 44) **0116 234 0205**

FUTURE PROMISE

Barbara Cowan

The huge problem of the sale of the garage, their home and livelihood, worried Morag Kinloch. Her father felt his only two options — be a taxi driver for a former apprentice or manage his estranged sister's business — demeaned him. Then the rumour about her young sister's new male lodger added to Morag's anxiety. So Gordon McEwan's reflections on their future had to wait.

RHAPSODY OF LOVE

Rachel Ford

When painter Maggie Sanderson found herself trapped in the same Caribbean hideaway as world-famous composer Steve Donellan, she was at a loss what to do. She tried to distance herself from him, but he seemed determined to make his presence felt, crashing his way around the house day and night. Was there no way she could find peace from this man, or was he going to ruin her sanity too, as he had ruined everything else?